HAVING HIS BACK

THE BRIDES OF PURPLE HEART RANCH BOOK 5

SHANAE JOHNSON

THOSE JOHNSON GIRLS

Copyright

PROLOGUE

Xavier picked his way over the dilapidated structures littering the patchy field. Interspersed with the discarded rubbish, rubble, and refuse of the junkyard there was broken concrete, dangling wire, and rotted wood. The place was a virtual landmine waiting to ensnare a booted heel, tennis shoe toe, or the instep of a flat heel. He stepped carefully to get through it in order to get to the treasure on the other side.

"Oomph."

Xavier turned, immediately on guard. In addition to the treasure he sought before him, there was precious cargo behind him. "You okay?"

Darkness cloaked them inside the fenced in land of rejected items. But Cassandra Butler was a bright ray of sunshine to his eyes. She had been since the first time he'd seen her walking down the street humming an old spiritual tune.

Xavier had stopped walking that day he'd first heard Cassie sing. Cars had honked interrupting her melodic song. He turned to shout at them to stop all the noise so that he could only hear her pure voice, only to realize he'd stopped walking in the middle of the street and the light was now green. Xavier had quickly crossed out of harm's way and trailed behind the songbird.

Cassie trailed behind him now, picking her way over scrap and debris in her sandals. He'd told her to dress practical for their date, but he supposed this was practical to Cassie. She wore a long sundress with a cardigan covering her shoulders.

As part of her religion, Cassie never wore pants. All her shirts were buttoned up, and if her shoulders shown, she covered them with a sweater in the cold months or a cardigan in the warm months. In the eight months they'd been dating, he'd never seen her bare shoulders. The sight of her bare toes in the sandals made his mouth water.

"I'm fine," Cassie said, wrapping her fingers around his bicep.

Just the touch of her fingers and the fact that she

was leaning on him for support made Xavier feel ten times stronger. He'd had his fair share of women before he'd turned twenty last year. Fast girls and loose women flocked to the dark haired boy with the golden brown skin, the gift of gab, and the mischievous twinkle in his light gray eyes.

Xavier had welcomed them all with wide open doors. Until that fateful day in the street when he'd been rendered immobile by this innocent, untouched, shoulder-covered songbird.

His gift of gab hadn't swayed Cassie when he'd caught up with her. She'd turned away from the twinkle in his gaze and looked down at the ground. But even worse, she'd stopped singing.

Xavier had followed, pursued was more like it. She'd given him one-word answers intent on dissuading any further communication. He was undaunted until she turned a corner that he didn't care to follow.

It was into a church. Xavier had nothing to say to God. But he wanted to talk to the girl again, and so he'd waited.

But after twenty minutes of waiting outside the church, her voice rose and called him inside. Xavier's feet moved before he'd thought about it. Inside the church, she'd stood out amongst a group of people, a choir. In the center of the choir, she shown bright singing the most beautiful song. Xavier had taken a seat in the back row.

He'd led many a girl astray in his young life. For the first time, a girl led him down a righteous path. She was like the sirens in the Greek myths. But instead of bashing his head into a rock, Cassie stole into his heart.

"We're almost there."

Xavier pulled her to him now. He kept Cassie close, urging her to walk in his footsteps as they made their way through the junkyard and to the surprise on the other side.

It had been weeks since he'd last seen her. Now he couldn't look his fill of her. His hands ached to span across her back, to hold her cheek. He wanted to bend down and taste her. But he held back.

As a man who'd never had to temper his appetite for the fairer sex, Cassie was a meal that was not on the menu. Surprisingly, that hadn't deterred him. Not even during their long absences from one another.

He lifted her up and over a discarded muffler. When her body pressed against his, part of him wanted to take advantage. But his heart cooled his carnal desires. Mostly.

She slid down his front as the temperature rose and his mouth watered. He allowed himself a small taste of her lips, savoring the sigh that escaped her perfect mouth as he pressed his advance. As he pulled her closer, her thigh pressed against the protrusion at the front of his pants.

Xavier placed her on the ground and cleared his throat. He put distance between them, not wanting her to question that particular bulge until the time was right. He'd been planning this night for weeks, and he wouldn't let anything go wrong.

He wrapped his right hand around her left, toying with the bare fingers of her left hand. He smiled under the cover of night with a secret she would soon know. If things went his way, that hand wouldn't be bare much longer.

In the clearing, they came to the place he'd wanted to show her. A white gazebo with lace trellis. The structure was like something out of a fairytale at the end of a dark and forbidding forest.

"Oh, Xavier," Cassie sighed. "It's beautiful."

At the other side of the gazebo was a field of wildflowers. Xavier led Cassie up the steps where he'd set up a blanket, a picnic basket, and a cell phone with speakers playing an old gospel tune. The singer was the only songstress who could rival Cassie's voice.

Cassie had introduced him to Evangeline Taylor's music. In the times when he couldn't hear her sing, Evangeline had kept him company. But the gospel singer was a pale comparison to his Cassie's voice.

Cassie glanced over the setup, but when she looked up and out, her mouth rounded into an awed O. Looking out over the gazebo, beyond the flowers, was a cliff where the Montana mountains met the stars.

Xavier came up behind her, wrapping his arms around her. "They say this is what it looks like out in the desert. You can see where the mountains meet the sky. This is the sky I'll be lying under and thinking of you for the next nine months."

She turned to him, a tear in her eyes. Cassie didn't like talking about his deployment. He'd first spied Cassie just a few weeks before he reported to Basic Training. They'd spent nearly every day together after she'd let her guard down. Then he was gone.

They weren't able to communicate. There was plenty of high technology like video chatting and email in the Army. But Cassie's strict parents didn't allow any of that. There was also plenty of low technology communications like phones and letters. But her parents had not approved of him the one and only time they'd met him.

So when Xavier left town for training, they had no contact. But he thought of her every day and night. She was surprised when, nine weeks later, he returned to find her. But once again, their time was short and he had to leave just a few weeks later for his Advanced Individual Training. The moment he was able to leave, he came running back to her.

And now that his training was complete, he had only a few days before he reported for his first deployment overseas. This time, they'd spend nine months apart. He didn't doubt that his feelings would increase in the long time span, and he needed her to know it. He had just the way to prove it to her and it was wearing a hole in his front pocket.

"I'm going to imagine you singing to me under this sky," he said.

"I will," she said. "I'll sing for you every night."

Xavier pressed his lips to hers. He'd kissed a lot of girls, but no one had ever been as sweet as Cassie. He'd dabbled in recreational drugs in the not too distant past. But after a taste of Cassie's lips, nothing ever gave him such a high, and he quit every substance. Except her.

"There's something else," he said when he pulled away from their kiss.

He led her to the blanket he'd laid out and the picnic basket. Cassie loved romantic things like this. She wasn't into jewelry and gifts like other girls. A simple walk in the park while talking, or a picnic and she would give him the biggest smile. Well, she was getting both tonight. The picnic and a piece of jewelry.

Xavier sat her down on the blanket. He fumbled in his front pocket, pulling out the box. Cassie gasped as she looked down at the jewelry encased inside.

"Cassie, I've never felt this way about another person in my life. You mean everything to me. The only reason I joined the army was because I didn't know what to do with my life. Then I met you."

She looked up at him with that twinkle in her eyes. The twinkle shone bright even as her eyes glistened in the moonlight. Xavier swiped the tears away. The drop fell into his hand and instantly evaporated at the center of his warm palm.

"When I come back, I'll be able to provide for you," he said as he presented the ring. It was a modest piece of jewelry he'd picked up from a pawn shop. The navy blue gem reminded him of Cassie's eyes. "You don't have to answer me now. I just need you to know what my plan is and that my intentions are-"

"Yes."

"Yes?"

She threw her arms around him, pulling him close, and squeezing him hard enough to elicit a cough.

Xavier caught her and held on. He didn't think it was possible to be this happy. But the happiness in his heart kept growing and growing. This little church girl, this preacher's daughter, had swept him off his feet and nearly knocked him on his back.

Cassie took the ring and aimed it for her left ring finger. But Xavier stopped her.

"You know your father won't approve now. Not when I have nothing to offer you but my word."

"Your word is good enough for me. I trust your word. I believe in you."

God, this woman. She was the reason Xavier began calling on God again. If He could bring such a perfect treasure into his life, then surely the higher power existed and was looking out for him.

"Xavier, I love you. Nothing my father says will ever change that."

"Cassie, I love you too. I'm going to prove myself worthy of you."

She shook her head and pressed a kiss to his lips. "You're already worthy of me. I am yours. Now and forever."

She pressed another kiss to his lips, deeper this time. Cassie's kiss was urgent and unending.

Xavier had learned to temper himself in the last two months. He'd never been without company since discovering the pleasures of a woman. He hadn't touched another woman since that first day he'd seen Cassie and heard her sing nearly a year ago.

When she'd allowed him to hold her hand, his body had ignited with desire. But he felt no urge to go further, no urge to press his suite. He would wait forever for this girl.

At the same time, he was still a man. Cassie's kisses were getting very insistent, and her body rubbed against his in a way he hadn't experienced for many, many months.

"Cass." He held her away taking a deep breath. "Slow down there."

She shook her head. "I don't see the need. You

just promised yourself to me forever. In the eyes of God, we're already married."

Xavier's breath caught as he looked down at this girl who'd stolen his heart and changed his life. She was right. Even though he was deploying in just a couple of days, the nine months they were about to spend apart wouldn't change anything in his heart. He was hers, and she was his.

Forever …

*our years later …*

"I'm sorry, Cassie, but there's nothing I can do. It's beyond my control."

Cassie Butler didn't even have the energy to sigh. Her shoulders were so used to being rigid that they didn't slump at the news. She barely even blinked her eyes because she was so tired that her eyelids couldn't be bothered to take the journey downward only to come back open at the top. So they simply stayed open as her boss delivered her the news.

"When is the store closing?" she asked.

"The lease is up at the end of the year, but I can't

afford to even stay that long. So I'll have to pay a penalty fee for breaking the contract. I have to close at the end of the month. I'm sorry, but that means I can only pay you for last week."

He looked devastated. Cassie knew she should offer him compassion. It's what her God-fearing parents would demand she do. Well, they'd demand she do it for strangers, but they'd offered no such compassion to their own daughter when she found herself in a bind.

It so happened that Cassie didn't have any compassion extra in store. She was too focused on her own plight to think of the fate of poor Mr. Adams and the record store he'd pumped money into during the age of digital downloads. Cassie was low on cash. She was out of a job. And she didn't have enough to cover next month's rent.

Nope. All she could think about was what was she going to do?

She couldn't go home to her parents. Those doors had closed four years ago when she'd discovered that she was pregnant out of wedlock. Her parents hadn't bought into the idea that He Who Shall Not Be Named had given her a ring and promised to marry her in nine months upon his return from deployment. Nine months had come and gone, and that person, whom she longed to forget, had never returned. She'd finally had to admit that she'd just been another notch on his bedpost.

Instead of showing her compassion, her parents had punished their youngest daughter for her poor decision making and loose morals. They'd sent her to a home for wayward girls who'd found themselves in a family way. Cassie hadn't been allowed to read the books, but she was sure the best way to describe Saint Agnes's House was akin to something out of a Victorian gothic novel, minus the locking girls in closets. But only barely.

Cassie had only spent a few nights in that house of horrors before running away to a women's shelter. She'd been living on borrowed time, borrowed beds, and borrowed couches ever since. Just once in her life, she wanted to feel secure once more. Be it in a home of her own, a room of her own, or even a bed with four posts and not a box spring on the floor.

None of those simple dreams would happen in this moment and this time. Her time here, just like her time at St. Agnes, and her time in the shelter and her time in various rented rooms was up. And just like all the other times, she'd find a way.

Her shoulders straightened even more. Her eyes

blinked once. But when they opened, she still didn't have a plan. What she knew for sure was that there was no use hanging around here. There was nothing left for her here at the record shop.

She'd thought she could earn money and dip her toe in her passion for secular music. But no. It was not meant to be.

She'd have to go back to retail or fast food work where she'd only make enough money to cover rent and childcare. But that was going to be her life, and she'd just need to suck it up. She'd made this bed of choices, and she would lie in it.

Forever.

Cassie stood and turned to go from the office. "Thank you for giving me a chance. I wish you the best."

After all, it wasn't Mr. Adams's fault that he'd taken a gamble on opening a record store that sold only gospel and secular music out in the middle of nowhere Montana when music could be downloaded to a phone or computer from the comfort of the modern consumer's phone. Cassie had had more far-fetched dreams herself, like believing the word of a soldier who likely had conquests all over the world. If he had even been a soldier. For all she knew, that could've been another one of his lies.

On the other side of Mr. Adams's door, Cassie looked down at where she'd left her daughter. The seat was empty. She didn't panic. Rebecca was at the front. She wouldn't' have let Alex go out the door. She was probably just walking around the stacks of music.

In one corner of the shop, Cassie spied a young boy frowning at the records as though he didn't know what they were. That was another reason the record store was going under. Aside from not listening to praise music, young kids listened to digitized music they could carry around in their pockets.

"Alexandra, where did you go? I told you to sit in the chair until mommy was finished with her meeting."

The only other person in the store was a tall man. He had golden skin and a dark head of hair. He held an album in his hands. Even from this distance, Cassie could tell that it was Evangeline Taylor's first album. She was surprised that someone so young, and a man at that, would be interested in the classics. It was likely for his great-grandmother. He was lucky he'd gotten the album since the store was going out of business. It wasn't an item an online retailer would easily have in stock.

The man was looking down, but as Cassie approached he looked up. Cassie was caught by the lightest gray eyes. Just like her daughter's. Just like …

Oh, no. Oh, no no no.

This could not be happening. She'd always told herself if she ever saw him again, she'd just cross the other street. She wouldn't confront him and be humiliated. She needed to find Alex and get out of there.

And then her worst nightmare came true. Her daughter was hanging on her father's legs, looking up at him like he'd hung the moon.

"Cassie?" He whispered her name as though it were an answered prayer.

"Xavier." She whispered his name like it was a punch to her gut.

Cassie took the steps toward him, careful not to touch any part of him as though he had the plague. She swooped up her daughter in her arms. Then she made a mad dash for the door as Xavier called her name again.

She'd parked at the curb outside of the store since it was her day off when Mr. Adams had called her in, and she hadn't planned to stay long. Wasn't that ironic. She was never coming back here.

She yanked open the back door of her car. Plunging Alex into her car seat, Cassie quickly strapped the three-year-old in. By the time she was done and hopping into the front seat, Xavier was on her.

Cassie slipped inside, closed the driver's side door, and shoved down the lock to his protests. She ignored them. She had to get out of here. She couldn't face more attacks on her dignity today. Her quota had been exceeded.

So, of course, her car decided it didn't want to start. She was trapped in her worst nightmare with the man she'd given her heart to on one side boxing her in, and a future that was leading nowhere in front of her. So she did what any sensible woman would do. She put her head down on the steering wheel and cried.

CHAPTER TWO

Xavier stood on the curb looking into the car. He stared so long that his gaze shifted, and instead of the distraught woman crying on the steering wheel, he saw his own dumbfounded reflection in the driver's side window.

The car looked like it had seen better days—a few decades ago. It was the color of rust with a few gray specks sprinkled in for good measure. There was a puddle of some kind of liquid seeping from its underside. Smoke emanated from under the hood. From what he could see on the inside, the interior was threadbare, and a few springs poked out from the fabric.

None of that penetrated more than the sounds of Cassie's cries. He'd seen her shed tears before. Every time he'd have to leave she tried and failed to hold back tears. But she'd never once cried hysterically with her whole body shaking and misery etched on her face.

His gaze went from Cassie crying in the front seat, to the baby girl, Alexandra, crying in the back seat. Through the glass that separated them, Alex held her arms out for him. Her gray eyes implored him to do something to make it stop, to make it better.

Xavier was rarely at a loss for words. This would be the top time of his life that he didn't know what to say. But there was something he could do.

He went to the passenger side of the car. It was unlocked. Xavier pulled the door closed behind him as he climbed inside.

Cassie lifted her face, tears staining her cheeks. Xavier couldn't look at her directly in the eyes. Instead, he reached over her.

She shrank back from him. Pressing her body into the driver's side door. Her hands curling over her chest as though she were protecting her heart.

He tried not to let her reaction get to him, but it did. This was the woman he had loved fiercely four years ago. If he were honest with himself, and he rarely was, he still loved her.

Cassandra Butler was the only woman he'd ever loved. The only one he probably could ever love. And he'd lost her to another man. Wherever that man was, Xavier wanted to punch him in the face for leaving his family in such a state.

For starters, this car was a death trap that shouldn't be allowed on the road. But even before that, Xavier had noticed that Alexandra's sundress was a size too small. Cassie's sweater was as threadbare as the seat cushions, and he could see her collarbones protruding just a tad too much.

But he couldn't think on any of that now. He had a mission to complete. Xavier reached down below the dash and pulled the lever to release the hood of the car. Still not looking at Cassie and trying to mute the sobs of the little girl in the back seat, he got out of the passenger side and lifted the hood.

Carlos stood on the sidewalk watching the entire scene with the curious eyes of a preteen. "What can I do?"

Fran would be proud of his adopted brother at that moment. That was exactly the right response. But Xavier didn't even know what he was supposed to do.

"Go to my truck and get the tools out of the back."

Carlos did as he was told as Xavier tried to solve the only problem he had any details on. The hood of the car blocked his view of Cassie. Pretty soon, the cries died down. But as Xavier looked at the mess of oil and wires under the hood, he still had no clue how to solve a single problem before him.

He'd tried for the last four years to get Cassie off his mind and out of his heart. Every night he failed as he dreamed about her. Every morning he failed as her voice sang in his daydreams. They had been apart for years, but every time he looked up at the night's sky, every time he saw a wildflower, she was never far from his thoughts.

And now here she was, with his child. It had to be his child. Those eyes. The feminization of his name.

Xavier closed the hood of the car and came around to the driver's side. He knocked on the window. He watched as Cassie took a deep breath to calm herself. Then she rolled the window down.

"Did you fix it?" she asked, looking ahead and not at him. The little girl sat on her lap. She turned sleepy eyes to Xavier and smiled. He noted that, along with the gray eyes and black hair, she had the same dimple on the right side of her cheek as he did.

"No. I can't fix it."

Alex held her hands out to Xavier. He lifted a finger and ran it down the side of her face. Her grin spread even wider as she gazed back at him.

"We need to talk," said Xavier.

"No need. I can get it towed back to my place."

There was a twitch in her jaw. Cassie wasn't a liar. At least not the Cassie he knew. The girl he'd known years ago believed lying was a sin. But when there was something she was trying to avoid, her lip would twitch, as though the full story was trying to come out, and she was trying to hold it back.

"Fine," he said. "We can talk while the tow truck comes."

She turned, facing him for the first time since their reunion, and glared at him.

"I think there might be some raised voices during this conversation," Xavier continued. "Maybe Alexandra should play with my friend, Carlos."

"I'm not giving my baby to a stranger."

"He's not a stranger. He's a good kid who lives on my ranch. I'd trust him ... with my life."

"I have a little sister," said Carlos, coming up behind Xavier and poking his head in the window. "I know how to entertain little girls."

Cassie looked from Carlos to Xavier, down to Alex, and back around again. Finally, she opened the door and passed Alex to Carlos. As the two went off and sat on a bench a few yards away, Xavier came around to the passenger side. He opened the door, climbed in, and sat down on the worn down seat.

They were quiet for a few moments. Partly because his back was uncomfortable in the seat. The one-year-old scars that covered his back warred with the springs of the seat.

The other part was because his body felt alive again for the first time in four years. He was sitting next to Cassie. But she wasn't in his arms. It felt wrong.

"Alex is what, three and a half?" Xavier asked.

Cassie didn't answer. She crossed her arms over her chest, making her collarbone look even more pronounced and her body emaciated. She'd been small when he'd known her before, but now she was painfully thin.

"She's mine, isn't she?"

Cassie turned and glared. "What? You think I'm the kind of girl to sleep around?"

"Cassie." Xavier held up his hands.

"You think that there were other guys after I promised you my heart and gave you my body?"

"I didn't say that."

"Then what were you trying to say asking if you were the father?"

"I was asking for confirmation."

"You know how the process works. You don't need me to teach you. Man lays with woman. Baby is produced."

Her nostrils were flaring. There was a sheen of sweat across her forehead. But her chin remained high.

Xavier could only stare. Who was this woman? It was not his sweet and gentile Cassie. There were dark lines around her eyes as though she weren't getting enough sleep. The creases of her mouth had frown lines. There was a paleness he didn't like along with the thinness to her. The last four years had been rough on her. Why hadn't she reached out to him? But more importantly, where was her husband? The man she'd married after she'd promised him her heart.

"I don't understand why you're so shocked," she continued. "I'm sure this isn't the first time you've had this conversation with a woman you've had a one-night-stand with."

"One-night-stand? I was going to marry you."

"You can drop the act now. It's been years. Besides, you got what you wanted, and I didn't come after you asking for anything. I'm not asking for anything now. You can go back to your philandering ways and leave me and my daughter alone."

"Our daughter."

"She's been your daughter for fifteen minutes."

"No. She's been my daughter for nearly four years, and you didn't tell me about it."

"You didn't come back for me."

"Yes, I did. I came back, and you were gone. Gone and married to someone else."

It still hurt to even say the words out loud. His Cassie, married to someone else just months after she'd promised to be his forever. But instead of the pain radiating from his heart and spreading through all his limbs, it stalled as he looked down at her.

Cassie was gaping at him as though he was speaking with a forked tongue. As though the words coming out of his mouth made no sense. The pain receded, and for the first time in four years, a spark of hope was kindled deep in his heart.

Maybe he had gotten it wrong? Perhaps he had been misinformed? Dear God, please let him be misled.

CHAPTER THREE

Cassie caught a glimpse of herself in the rearview mirror of her car. There were tears running down her face. Her nose was red. And her lips were trembling.

She was a mess.

She'd sworn never to let another person see her like this. She'd held it together inside the music store as she was being told she'd lost her job. She'd held it together when her parents had sent her packing from the only home she'd ever known. She'd held it together while she'd been in shelters where she wasn't guaranteed a bed every night.

She'd held it together when she'd gone looking for Xavier at the place he'd called his home only to have the people there laugh in her face about her predicament. Nine months after he'd left her, just a few days before she was due to give birth, she made her way to the inner city row homes he'd said he'd lived in but never took her to visit. The neighborhood had been as rough as he'd said, but by that time in her life, Cassie had seen worse as she bounced from group homes and shelters.

The family she'd found inside had no idea who she was, where he was, or what she expected them to do for her. Xavier had been back and was long gone, with plans to never return is what they told her. They also mocked that she wasn't the first girl to come looking for him because he'd promised them something.

It had been the last bastion of hope that she'd held onto. She left with her head high and her hands raw. There was nothing left to hold onto.

She'd cried her eyes out that night and went into labor the next day. She'd stopped looking for anyone to offer her help the moment she'd held Alex in her arms. She knew that no one would have her back but herself. And she'd sworn that if ever she came face to face with Xavier Ramos again, she'd tell him off without a care.

And now she was trapped in her broken down car with him and bawling her eyes out as he questioned the parentage of their child. Just the perfect end to this nightmare of a day.

"You didn't come back for me," she accused.

"Yes, I did," Xavier insisted, but Cassie wasn't truly listening to him.

Xavier had always been able to spin tall tales and tell fanciful stories to get her to smile. It was how he'd wormed his way into her heart and other places. She wouldn't fall for it again. She just needed to get him out of her car so that she could get home and cry. Though she wouldn't have long to cry in her tiny studio apartment. Rent was due in a couple of weeks. Even if she got another job, she wouldn't get paid in time.

"I came back, and you were gone."

More lies. She'd been there day he'd told her he was coming back. She'd gone first to the airport and waited for arrivals the entire day. Thinking she might have somehow missed him, she turned up at his family's house later that night.

It was all just more lies. She wasn't the naive girl he'd seduced all those years ago. She had been toughened up by the real world, and it took more than a charming grin and pretty words to get close to her these days. In fact, she hadn't gotten close to anyone since that one and only night with Xavier.

She just couldn't bring herself to trust another man.

"Gone and married to someone else."

That caught her attention. Married? To someone else? Exactly what did he think of her?

She felt her chest tighten as she glared at him. She wanted to shout at him, but her jaw was stiff. Her belly roiled with contempt.

Even after all he'd promised her, after everything she'd given to him, how could he believe that she would make vows to another man?

"I got a few days early leave after five months, and I came looking for you, to surprise you. Your parents told me you were gone. That you'd gotten married, moved away, and was expecting your first child."

Cassie could believe that. She knew her parents had concocted a story about her leaving the parish just as she'd begun to show. None of that was true. But she didn't want to get into any of the truth of the last four hellish years of her life with the man who had consigned her to her fate.

"Where's your husband?" asked Xavier.

Cassie glared at him. When she'd told her parents that she and Xavier had been married under God, they asked her the same question. Over and again for three months until they couldn't hide her sin any longer. When they could no longer hide her shame, they sent her away.

"You're not wearing a ring," said Xavier.

Cassie balled her left hand into a fist. She shoved the lack of evidence down into the seat cushion. Her hand met with the metal of the worn fabric of her old car.

"Either he's gone," said Xavier. "Or he never was there to begin with."

"You got that right," Cassie muttered, her gaze narrowed, pointing all accusations at the man before her.

"Why didn't you wait for me, Cassie?"

"I couldn't."

"Why not? Was it your parents?"

A vein throbbed in her forehead, threatening to burst and spill all the thoughts she was trying to keep to herself. She pressed her lips together, but they trembled. She bit her lower lip, but it still opened and her every pain and sorrow gushed out like the waters of a broken dam.

"I can't," she said. "I just can't do this right now. Can you just stop, please? I just need this day to stop. My car is dead. I lost my job. I can't make next month's rent. And now here you are. They say God doesn't give you more than you can handle, but my plate is full. So, can you just stop?"

He did. Xavier turned away from her and faced front. They sat in the car in silence for five glorious minutes.

They both looked out of the passenger side window at Carlos playing with Alexandra. The little girl was grinning up at him as though he were her new favorite toy. Soon, Alex's eyes were dropping. Carlos lifted her, brought her into the cradle of his arm, and began to rock her. Pretty soon the toddler was asleep.

Cassie wished she could hire the kid as a babysitter. Alex didn't take to too many people. But she'd immediately taken to this Carlos and her father.

"Is he your kid?" Cassie asked.

"No. He's one of my brothers' kids."

"I thought you were an only child."

"I am. I mean one of my Army brothers."

He sat erect, keeping his back off the cushions of the passenger seat. Cassie had never had occasion to sit in that seat, but she'd seen the inner metalwork peeking out anytime she sat groceries there. A part of her got a bit of satisfaction knowing he was in some discomfort.

But that satisfaction soon gave way. Cassie was gazing up at him. Xavier was looking down at her. His gray gaze was so full of concern. She remembered him looking at her with what she had believed was love in his eyes.

Her traitor heart flipped, and she turned away. The sudden move had the metalwork of the driver's seat pressing into her spine. Good, she needed that jolt of pain to remind her of what might happen to her if she let down the guarded wall she'd built around her heart.

"I have to go," she said.

"Where?"

She didn't answer.

"You're coming home with me."

Cassie shook her head and reached for the door handle. "The last time I went anywhere with you I wound up pregnant and alone. I'm not going down that road again."

"Cassie." He didn't raise his voice. But the command in it made her stop. "You're going to tell me where you live. We're getting your things. And then you and my daughter are coming home with me."

Cassie opened her mouth to argue. But nothing came out. The truth was, she had no clue as to what she was going to do next. She had no money, no transportation, and the roof over her head was about to be pulled away. She couldn't go back to another shelter.

She turned to face Xavier. His features were set into a stern look that broke no argument. Cassie didn't have the energy to argue. She didn't know which way to turn. For one moment, it would be nice if someone else took charge of her disaster of a life.

Xavier owed her this much. It would just be for a moment. Then she'd figure out what to do on her own because she certainly couldn't trust him to keep his word.

CHAPTER FOUR

Xavier pulled up behind the tow truck lugging Cassie's car. The truck stopped at the address that Cassie had given. She tugged at the door handle from the back seat of his truck, but it was locked. Xavier had half a mind to keep it that way.

He thought he'd grown up in a rough neighborhood. This place made his old stomping ground look like an oasis. There were boards in many of the windows in the apartment complex. Graffiti covered the brick. And he was sure he just saw a drug deal go down between two adolescents.

He unlocked his door, then went around to Cassie's side. Before he could hand her out, she already had a sleeping Alex in her arms and was stepping onto the sidewalk. Everything in him urged Xavier to march in front of the two to protect them both. But he had to deal with the tow truck driver first.

The driver lowered Cassie's car to the street. Behind Cassie's back, Xavier paid the guy to come back tonight and tow the heap to the junkyard. There was no way either Cassie or Alex would ever get in that death trap again.

They also wouldn't be coming back to this dilapidated structure that someone was trying to pass off as living quarters. Once inside the building, his nightmares got worse as roaches reigned free. The stench burned his nostrils. The sounds made a seasoned soldier like him jerk and jump.

Inside her apartment was no better. His stomach hurt and the scars at his back tugged to think that they'd been living in this filth. The apartment was mostly bare. Other than a few toys littered around the room, there was only a mattress laid atop a box spring on the floor. Clothes were spilling out of a worn suitcase. A small square television sat on a metal chair, bunny ears protruding from the top at odd angles.

"Gather up everything," Xavier instructed Carlos.

Xavier tried to keep his face nonjudgmental, but

he was judging. She'd rather live like this than reach out to him? He turned to Cassie. She was rocking Alex who was wavering between waking up and falling back to sleep.

"Do your parents know you live here?" he asked.

"I don't know where my parents are." Her gaze never left the child whose eyes finally decided to close instead of remain open. Alex settled back in the crook of her mother's neck and began breathing evenly and softly. "We haven't spoken since Alex was born. Last I heard, they left town out of shame for their unwed daughter who got knocked up by a forked-tongue sinner."

Her head was high in defiance, but her shoulders looked like they would break if just one more piece of straw landed on them. Xavier decided not to fight her perceptions of him. He'd have them too if he'd had to live like this.

He had had to live in his own version of hell these past four years. War had taken a pound of flesh from him. It was a pain he deserved. Cassie hadn't been the only casualty of his ability to persuade people.

That last night with Cassie hadn't been about persuasion. He truly would've waited for her, as long as she wanted. He didn't need to remind her that she was the one who'd pressed for more.

In the war, he hadn't had time to wait to get what he wanted. Xavier had been trained in strategic communications in the army. His persuasive abilities had gotten him bits of information that was necessary for his unit to function and the army's mission to progress.

In his last deployment, he'd gained the trust of an informant and got information that was crucial to finding and taking down targets. But there was always collateral damage. That collateral damage showed up the next day as a child suicide bomber took out his unit and the community they'd been building.

Lives were lost that day. Luckily, no one from his unit was buried that day. Still, scars were formed that never truly healed.

The skin on his back pulled as he hefted Cassie's suitcase down the stairs. Xavier had gotten used to his scars. But he still walked around in hell every day. And now his angel was back, standing before him, and he couldn't reach out to her.

Four years ago, when he'd accumulated a couple days leave during his training, he leaped at the chance to get back to Cassie. His thought had been to surprise her, but also just to be near her. To hold the woman he considered his wife in his arms. To hear her melodic voice sing to him, speak to him. Instead, he was left sucker punched in his heart, and his throat seized.

He'd always known he wasn't good enough for Cassie. His every thought, his every action since the day he'd met her had been to make himself worthy of her. The only way he knew to be respectful was to serve.

But that wasn't good enough for her parents. They'd turned their noses up at him the one time Cassie had introduced him. They'd sneered when he'd turned up on their doorstep in uniform. He was certain they took some satisfaction in delivering the news that Cassie was married and expecting.

But it was a lie. It was all a lie. There was no husband. But there was a baby. His baby.

With all of their worldly possessions packed in a suitcase and trash bags, he packed them in the truck, fastening a sleeping Alex securely in her car seat. Cassie hopped in the back beside their daughter while Carlos took the front seat. The drive back to the ranch was in silence as everyone eventually fell asleep.

The quiet was welcome as it gave Xavier time to

think. The one thing he knew for certain was that now that he had Cassie back, he was never letting her out of his sight again. He knew just the way to make sure she'd be with him until the end of time. He just had to convince her to say yes again.

He looked at Cassie and Alex asleep in the back of his truck.

He may not be the man she deserved to have, but he was the one she had, and he would not let her down. Not ever again.

If she took his hand, in earnest this time, he could offer them a home, security. Maybe even one day she might come to love him again because he had never stopped loving her.

CHAPTER FIVE

In her dreams was the only time Cassie found peace. That and watching Alex sleep. But whenever Alex closed her eyes, Cassie was always right behind her, and then the dream would start.

It was a simple dream. She wasn't flying. She wasn't rich from winning the lottery. She didn't have magical powers and could become invisible.

No, there was nothing magical about the dream. In it, she just wasn't alone anymore. She didn't have all the constant weight and pressure on her shoulders.

Still, Cassie hated the dream. The reason why? Xavier was there.

In the dream, he had one arm around her

shoulder tucking her into the nook between his chest and chin. He held Cassie's cheek in the other hand, tilting her face up for a feather-light kiss. He looked at her with love in his eyes and spoke words of adoration.

"There's no rush." Those were the only words he ever said to her. That and the three little words that made her heart skip beats even while she was asleep.

After the kisses and the sweet words, they would turn and observe their surroundings. They had a small house, nothing fancy. A small yard. Two bedrooms, one for them and one for Alex. The rooms were all furnished with nice furniture, no hand me downs or worn furnishings. And in each bedroom was a four-poster bed up off the floor where bugs couldn't join them.

Cassie was happy in the dream. She had no worries. She was cared for. She could sing, and her heart wouldn't be heavy. She hadn't sung a happy song in so long. But she did in her dreams.

Oh, how she hated the dream. Because every morning she'd wake up. And then it was back to her bleak reality.

She was being jostled awake now. Her eyes jerked open. Her first thought was Alex. She reached over to the car seat to find it empty. Panic slammed into her chest.

"She's fine," said a calming voice. "She's right over there."

Cassie sat up and followed the trajectory of the finger pointing out the window. She saw Alex waddling along with Carlos who held her small hand in his. A young girl with the same dark hair as Carlos had her arms open wide as she bent down to Alex. To Cassie's surprise, Alex went right into the girl's embrace without a fuss. Her little was never this familiar with strangers.

Where was she? Who were these people? What was this place?

Cassie turned back to face Xavier. He was standing over her. He was so close she could smell his cologne. It was the same brand he'd worn years ago. She hated the comfort that washed over her. She wanted to curl into his chest and bury her face into his chest. Instead, she strong-armed him away from her.

"Where are we? Where did you bring us?"

She stepped out of the truck and into a slice of heaven. There was green as far as the eye could see. Where the green pastures ended, the mountains began. In the distance, she saw men riding horses at a trot. Goats mulled around a fenced in enclosure. A burst of color beyond that hinted at a flower garden. When she turned to look behind her, she saw that she stood in the driveway of a row of quaint cabins all gathered in a semi-circle.

"Welcome to Purple Heart Ranch," said Xavier. "It's a rehabilitation ranch for wounded vets."

"You were wounded?" Her hand rose, as though reaching out to comfort him. As soon as the words came out of her mouth, she wished she could shove them away. She didn't care that he was wounded. She shoved her hand in her pocket and looked away from him.

Xavier nodded but didn't elaborate. "This is my home."

He waved his hand in front of a small one story home. It could've come out of Cassie's dreams. There was a small patch of yard. A rocking chair sat on the porch. A small flower bed lay off to the side of the house.

With her suitcase in hand, Xavier climbed the few steps and opened the front door. Cassie noted that the door was unlocked, something she hadn't done in the last four years. She stepped inside the open door and had to pick her jaw up off the floor.

She had to be dreaming. Because this was the

home she'd been dreaming of for the last four years. Down to the flowery lace on the couch cushions.

There was a sofa, with not only couch cushions, but a crocheted throw. A coffee table sat in front of the sofa along with two plush chairs. Tucked in the corner was a record player. Over top of the old fashioned stereo was a library of records. Cassie itched to thumb through them, certain she'd find many of her favorite modern gospel records and old spiritual recordings.

When they'd first began seeing each other, she'd turned Xavier onto gospel. They spent many evenings sitting in his car and listening to music. Sometimes, she'd sing to him. Other times, she simply sat in his embrace while the speakers crooned to them. By the end of their year together, he'd amassed quite a hall. She was sure all those records were there, with many more added.

"There's two bedrooms. You and Alex can have this one."

Cassie followed as Xavier led her down a short hall. Two doors faced one another. Before going into the room he indicated, she stole a glance into the opposite room—his room. There was a large king-sized bed with a dark comforter. The headboard was made of intricate woodwork. Another record player sat on a nightstand on one side of the bed. The album cover leaning on the record player was by one of her favorite singers, a singer she'd introduced him to.

She turned from his room and looked into the room he indicated would be hers. The bedroom was bigger than the studio apartment she'd just vacated. The bed was on a four-poster frame with clean sheets and a bright comforter. There was a dresser and a closet big enough to house everything she came with and room for more.

It was perfect. Just like a dream. "What's the catch?"

Cassie rounded on Xavier as he put her luggage into the room. He scratched at the back of his neck, not quite meeting her gaze for a moment. When he did, she saw that there was something hidden in his gaze.

"I've learned over the last four years that nothing in this world is free," she said. "What do you want? What do I have to give you for staying here?"

Gray eyes gazed down upon her. Cassie had once thought she could read Xavier. She knew when he was exaggerating and when he was telling her the honest truth. She knew when he was trying to hide his sadness or shame and when he was truly happy.

Shame and vulnerability mixed with resolve in his gray gaze now. Whatever he was about to say, she knew she didn't want to hear it. She knew she wouldn't like it.

"The ranch is zoned for families," he began. "You and Alex can stay as long as you want. Forever, in fact."

She waited, certain the proverbial bomb had yet to drop. Xavier licked his lips, holding onto his bottom lip with his teeth a second before letting it go and detonating this fantasy world he'd brought her into.

"You'll just have to marry me," he said.

"Marry you?"

Her stomach dropped into her toes. In all her imaginings about coming face to face with Xavier Ramos again, she never imagined this scenario.

CHAPTER SIX

"Marry you? Because of zoning?"

Xavier hesitated. The zoning issue was a convenient excuse. But the truth was he'd been ready to pack his bags and leave the ranch at the end of the week when his time was up. He'd never planned to marry anyone else because, in his heart, he was already married. And then, he'd been blessed with another glimpse of his wife.

"Oh," Cassie sighed. Those navy blue eyes darkened with a cold cynicism. "I get it. This isn't about me. It's about you. In order for you to stay here, you have to get married, and I'm just convenient."

"Cassie, no—" But he faltered.

Though the blue of her eyes was on the darker

spectrum, Xavier had always regarded them as sapphire gems. They'd always reflected light back at him. Never once since he'd known her had Cassie's eyes been filled with distrust and contempt.

He wanted to tell her that he still loved her. That he'd never stopped. But the dark shade of her gaze told him that she wouldn't hear him.

"I'll do it," she said. "I'll marry you. I'll move in."

Reeling wasn't exactly the right word to describe the twist and turn of his emotions. His heart pounded in his chest. But the cold that he felt in his fingertips and toes let him know it was not a happy occasion.

"But this is just a marriage of convenience," she continued. "My convenience. I'm no longer that fool girl who believed a man would sweep her off her feet. This will be a purely business arrangement. Not even platonic, because we're not friends. This will be the last time you use me, do you understand?"

There was no triumph in his gaze as he regarded her. All he felt was shame. What had happened to the joyous creature he'd left all those years ago? Whatever it was, it was his fault.

"Do we have a deal?" she said.

Cassie held out her hand to him. Xavier stared at her slim fingers. It was the same hand he'd held in his. The same hand he'd planted chaste kisses on. The same hand he'd clutched to his heart when she'd agreed to marry him the first time.

Shaking it now he felt dirty. But it was a means to an end. Xavier had talked people into and out of many things. He'd gotten people to divulge information without them realizing it. He'd droned on, planting seeds, until someone thought that his idea was theirs. When he turned on the charm, he always got what he wanted.

Xavier wanted to be in Cassie's life. But not in the way she'd just outlined. His hand felt clammy after clasping with hers to seal the deal she'd outlined.

But what other choice did he have? He couldn't let Cassie and his daughter go back to the squalor he'd taken them from. And now that he'd seen her again and knew that she was available, he'd do anything to get her back into his life. And then there was Alex.

"It's lunchtime," said Cassie. "I need to go get Alex. She's not very good with strangers."

They looked out the bedroom window. The view gave them a clear sight into Fran's front yard. Across the yard, Alex was the center of attention of the small crowd gathered. She had a huge grin on her face as she petted Maggie's dog.

Star, a pug with a face only a mother could love, laid her head in Alex's lap to the child's absolute delight. Alex ran her chubby hands up down the patchy skin on Star's back. Maggie had told them that Star had had a skin disease that caused hair loss. Alopecia, she'd called it. Xavier had felt a special kinship to the dog as their backs looked alike, with skin missing in spots.

"It looks like she's fine," said Xavier. "Would you like to come out and meet everyone?"

Cassie stepped back from the window. She crossed her arms over herself, as though she were protecting her heart, and shook her head. Xavier couldn't help but notice the dark circles under her eyes. Despite her fire a moment ago, she looked exhausted.

"Tell you what," he said. "Why don't I watch Alex for a while, and you can settle in here?"

She eyed him skeptically.

"You've been doing this on your own for four years. I can take the afternoon shift. Why don't you take a minute and get settled? There's food in the fridge. You can take a nap. When you're ready, I'll introduce you to everyone."

Cassie swallowed. Xavier watched her throat as

the lump passed through. Her shoulders relaxed slightly. One arm released its hold.

"She's allergic to dairy," Cassie said finally. "She doesn't like meat."

Xavier frowned at that. He was a carnivore down to his bones.

"It's a textural thing. Alex is special needs. She's nonverbal. And she's small for her age."

"There are doctors on the ranch," said Xavier. "They can see her and give us some help with any issues she has."

"I didn't do anything wrong," said Cassie. Her hands were balled into tight fists at her side. That chin went sky high again.

"I didn't say you did. I'm sure you did the best you could under the circumstances."

Circumstances he'd left her in. But if he'd known, he would've left the army entirely. He would've gone AWOL to be with his family. He would've been at her side every step of the way.

He wished he could reach out to her now. Take her in his arms and hold her and let her know that everything would be okay from this moment on. But he knew she wouldn't let him.

Cassie had never been a prideful person. But

there was a hardness to her now. A toughness that didn't suit her soft features.

Cassie crossed her arms over her chest and turned on her heel to go into the kitchen. Xavier had the urge to go to her and make her a plate, but he knew that wouldn't be appreciated either. He didn't have her trust.

But he had another little woman to make up time for. Xavier opened the front door and headed next door to Fran's. When he entered the yard, Eva and Maggie were both cooing over his little girl. When Alex saw Xavier, she made a beeline for him, arms outstretched, smile wide.

Xavier bent down and scooped the little girl up in his arms. He'd thought nothing could top his love for Cassie. But this little bundle of joy made his heart feel like it would burst.

Alex wrapped her arms tightly around him, as though she knew exactly who he was. That she was a part of him and now they were back together and whole.

"I always knew one day a woman would show up with a bundle of joy with your name on it."

He turned to face Dylan, the leader of his squad. The man regarded Xavier and his daughter with interest.

His daughter. He had a child. He was a father. He should be feeling overwhelmed. But all he felt was grateful, blessed, thankful that he'd found them when he did.

"I just never expected you to take in the mom as well."

"It's Cassie," said Xavier.

Dylan's brows rose. "The Cassie?" He whistled. "And that's clearly your kid."

Xavier rounded on his friend and leader. "Of course it's my kid. What are you saying about Cassie?"

Dylan held up his hands in defense. "You said she'd married someone else."

"Turns out it was a lie. Her parents told me that. They just wanted me out of her life. If I'd known …"

He pulled Alex in, resting his nose in the soft curls of her hair. She smiled up at him and placed a kiss on his cheek. Xavier's heart squeezed.

"I see you've moved her in," said Dylan. "So, it looks like you're staying? You're not taking on any contractor work any time soon?"

Xavier had applied for several overseas military contract jobs. His communication skills were a prized commodity, and he knew he wouldn't find any trouble getting work. He just hadn't cared to look while he was in residence on the ranch.

The money he received from the Army was enough for his bachelor life. But now that there were three mouths to feed, he'd have to consider other options. Perhaps some contract work in the states. But he didn't care to think about any of that now with Alex toying with his nose.

"I suppose there will be a wedding this weekend?" said Dylan.

"Yeah." Xavier sighed.

"Why aren't you happy about it?"

"She thinks I used her. She thinks I don't care about her."

"Is that all?" Dylan clapped him on his shoulder cap, careful to avoid his scarred back. "You've got a lifetime to prove her wrong."

That was true. When he'd said those vows the first time, he'd meant every one of them. This time he'd make it legal, and no one and nothing would tear them apart. He'd talked her into loving him once. He could do it again.

CHAPTER SEVEN

From the living room window, Cassie watched Xavier with his friends. The women smiled up at him, but not in a flirty way. In a friendly, we care about you way. The guys laughed with him and bumped shoulders with him. Five small dogs ran about his feet. The two children looked up at him as though he hung the moon. And then there was Alex.

Alex was cradled in his arms. She grinned up at him. She touched his face. She kissed his cheek. And all the while, Xavier held her to his chest like she was precious.

Cassie ached to be in her daughter's position. She ached to have Xavier look down at her with adoration. She ached to be surrounded by people who cared about her and her wellbeing. Even as Alex squirmed and jostled about in his arms, Cassie knew Xavier would never let their little girl fall. And if somehow Alex got loose, there was a small army of people surrounding him as back up.

Cassie turned away from the window with a sob in her throat and an ache in her heart.

Her community in the church had shunned her when she'd started seeing Xavier. Her parents had cast her out when they'd found out she was pregnant. The friends she thought she had hadn't come to her aide when she'd escaped the home her parents packed her off to. She'd been left alone.

Cassie wasn't sure she could ever put her trust in another person ever again. Looking in the fully stocked fridge, her stomach grumbled. For the past four years, she could never afford to fully stock one shelf of a refrigerator. Looking in at all the fare, she didn't think she could eat a thing. Her stomach was in too many knots.

She looked away from the kitchen and back down the hall to her bedroom. That soft mattress and clean comforter called to her. But she knew she definitely couldn't sleep. She was far too anxious about the deal she'd just struck with Xavier.

Marriage? A real one this time. Not a doomed promise under a starry sky.

Cassie turned from the comfort of her new home and slipped out the back door. She slunk around the side of the house so as not to be seen by anyone. Once certain no one had seen her, she walked a path, entirely directionless. The ranch was beautiful. It was the place she'd always dreamed of raising a family.

She came to a railing where horses roamed free. She leaned against the railing. She couldn't remember the last time it had been this silent. Nights in the shelters were filled with cries, groans, and snores. Nights in her apartment were filled with shouts, moans, and gunshots. The silence and tranquility of this place unnerved her. With no one around, she opened her mouth and sang a song.

She sang softly, quietly, not wanting to be heard by anyone but herself. But her voice rose an octave as she came to the crescendo of the song. As she let the final note trill from her tongue, the silence settled around her again. But it wasn't so daunting anymore.

"That was simply lovely, my dear."

Cassie turned to find an old man smiling at her.

His features called from a foreign land, India most likely.

"I'm sorry," she said. "I didn't mean to disturb you."

"You brightened my day. I would say that God gave you a gift with that voice, but clearly, it was a present to Himself so that he could hear you sing."

A smile tugged at Cassie's lips. She was typically suspicious of anyone, having been burnt so many times in the last four years with people meaning her well and then abandoning her. But something about this man, and the way he kept his distance set her at ease.

"They say when we sing, we are giving God his breath back." He tilted his head up to the sun and smiled brighter. "Unfortunately, God decided to fill me with my own breath. I can't carry a tune, I'm afraid."

A small tinkle of laughter reached her ears. Cassie was surprised to find it was her own laughter. How long had it been since she'd laughed with someone other than Alex?

"I've heard that song before," he said. "I can't remember where."

"It's a very old gospel song. I like old hymns."

"I know a young man who loves old hymns as

well. I catch him singing them often while he's working the fields. He prefers an audience of one, like you."

Cassie assumed he was talking about Xavier. There weren't many young men who preferred old secular music these days. In her recent neighborhood, all she ever heard was the grinding sound of electronically synthesized beats and shouting.

"I used to sing at my father's church." She had no idea why she said that.

Cassie opened her mouth, but then closed it. She'd been about to tell him more of her story. She didn't tell her problems to anyone anymore. Not even God. But she felt the urge to bare her soul to this quiet, old man.

"Your eyes lit up just then," he said, wagging a finger at her. "You clearly loved it. But I get the feeling you don't sing there anymore?"

"I moved away from home a long time ago."

"If you're in town, I would be honored if you would visit my church and add your voice to our choir."

It had been years since Cassie had been to church. She'd gone while she was pregnant, and a few times after Alex was born. She soon grew tired of the questions about where her husband was and the looks of disapproval. Something about this man told her she would get no such looks from him or his congregation.

"Are you local?" he asked.

"I am now. I just moved here. On to the ranch."

"On to the ranch?" His brows rose. "Are you by any chance a friend of Xavier Ramos?"

Cassie grimaced. She wouldn't call Xavier a friend. But he was about to be her husband.

The man chuckled. "Say no more, my dear. You must be Cassandra?"

"How did you know my name?" She advanced on him, coming to stand in front of him.

He extended his hand. "My name is Dr. Patel. I'm also Xavier's pastor."

"His Pastor? Xavier never went to church."

"Maybe not the man you knew."

"And you know about me because he … talked about me?"

Again the man smiled. "You know I can't reveal those details."

But in a way he already had. It was the only way Pastor Patel would know her name. What had Xavier said about her?

It didn't matter. Even if he'd told other people

about her, it was probably to confess his sins toward her. She would still guard her heart against him.

"What I can say is that I am very glad you're here," said Pastor Patel. "For his sake as well as yours. Now each of your healing can truly begin."

CHAPTER EIGHT

Xavier stood in the bedroom door staring down at his daughter. She was so peaceful in her sleep, much like her mother had been when she'd fallen asleep in his car. When they'd dated, he'd driven them out to the countryside on long drives. Cassie would always fall asleep in the passenger seat. He'd gotten into the habit of pulling over and just staring at her.

She'd always awaken, embarrassed. He'd simply kiss away any mortification she might have felt at being watched. On the drive home, she'd fall asleep again, and they'd repeat the process.

And then there was the night they spent together where she'd slept in his arms. He hadn't slept a wink that night, so enraptured was he of the woman who had given her heart, her body, and her soul to him. And this is what that night had produced; Alex.

Xavier had a plan to get himself and Cassandra back on a long and winding path where she'd trust him enough to fall asleep in his arms. He'd rehearsed the words in his head. He knew the moves he was going to make. He was just waiting for Cassie to return.

The sun had started to set thirty minutes ago. Sean had told him he'd seen Cassie walking near the pond an hour ago. Xavier had decided to let her have as much time to herself as she needed. But he was getting anxious.

He tried to tell himself he'd gone years without seeing her. But the last two hours without her were pure torture. Even though he knew she was on the grounds, he ached to be near her.

Finally, the front door opened and closed. Xavier held himself still. Even though everything in his being told him to go to her, he didn't. He let her come to him.

Cassie's soft footsteps got nearer to him. His heart kicked at his chest, reverberating on down to his ribs. Cassie came up to his back, though he knew it was Alex she was coming for.

Xavier felt Cassie's heat at his back. Instead of the pulls and tugs of the scarred skin there, he felt a soothing warmth. Xavier didn't like for anyone to touch his back, but if Cassie had chosen to place her hand there, he'd be in heaven. Of course, she didn't.

"She's asleep?"

"Yeah," he said, making space for Cassie in the doorway to the bedroom she would share with their daughter.

Cassie didn't go inside. She leaned against the opposite post and stared down at their little angel. Xavier wished the frame was smaller so that he could accidentally brush against her forearm. But Cassie had turned sideways, so there was no way an accidental touch would happen. He truly had his work cut out for him.

"She had potatoes and broccoli," said Xavier. "The broccoli made me doubt that she was my child."

His chuckle died when he looked over to find Cassie glaring up at him. Too soon for jokes. Got it.

"And she ate her weight in blueberries. There's a bush out back, and she picked them herself with Carlos and Rosalee's help. Those are the kids next door. They're already in love with her. And Eva and Maggie said they'll babysit whenever you need."

Cassie turned and walked away from him mid-sentence. She walked back into the living room, to the mantelpiece where photos of him sat. She ran her fingers over the picture frames. They were mostly pictures of him in the service with his squad. Curiously, she picked up a picture of him and Dr. Patel.

"You told your pastor about me?"

"I told everyone about you," he said. "About the songbird with the sweetest voice I'd ever heard."

She placed the picture frame down and moved onto his records. She fingered his cardboard coverings of the vinyl. Still sitting in the storage bag was the album he'd picked up today. That particular album, he'd searched years for.

"I'm the one that found this when the order came into the store," she said. "I should've known then."

The record was the one they'd listened most to on their drives, including the night they shared together. She shoved the album back inside the paperboy until the artwork was covered.

"So, this is where you've been the last few years?" she asked.

"The last year, yes."

She nodded, as she continued perusing various items in the room. Xavier kept a close watch on her features. The lines on her face told him she wasn't happy. He figured she thought he'd been living in the lap of luxury while she'd been struggling in something worse than poverty. But it hadn't been that way at all.

"Before that, I was in a hospital," he said, "recovering from my injuries. Before that, I did back to back tours in Afghanistan. I only came home the one time."

She glanced up at him. But only briefly, before she turned her back on him.

"The one time when I was looking for you." Then he asked the question he dreaded, but he needed to know. "Where were you?"

"My parents sent me to a home for sinful little girls who fornicated outside of wedlock and got pregnant." She grinned, but there was no humor in her voice. "When I got away from that horrible place, I went to your family. They said you'd come and gone. They laughed at me. Said I wasn't the only woman who'd come looking for you."

"They lied. Well, they misled you." There had been other women before her. None that had gotten pregnant, he'd been careful. He'd only lost his mind when he'd had her in his arms. "I came for you, Cassie."

"Well, you came too late. Or too early. Or whatever. The fact is you weren't there when I needed you. And now I don't need you."

She lifted that defiant chin. He would've believed her, if not for the tired lines around her eyes and the sag of her shoulders. She needed him. She needed him bad, and he would do everything in his power to convince her of that.

"It's not too late for us," he said, taking a step toward her.

Cassie held out her hands like a crossing guard halting traffic. "Don't you dare. Don't you come near me."

"You know I would never hurt you."

Her hands dropped, and she laughed at that, a full belly laugh that hurt Xavier's ears. "You couldn't do anything else to hurt me."

Xavier kept his distance, studying the movements of this target. Because she was the sole mark he was aiming for. With her square in his bullseye, he came to a realization. Like a hunter reading the signs left behind by his prey, Xavier saw all the hallmarks.

The anxiety, the mistrust. The sleep deprivation. The aim for emotional detachment. The hostility and the need for social isolation. Those were the hallmarks of PTSD.

As a soldier, he was trained to recognize the signs and to deal with them in his fellow comrades. He knew better than to convince her to feel a different way. To just stop feeling hurt and betrayal. To tell her that things were about to change for the better. Even though all of that was true. But that couldn't be his approach. He'd have to do this by the book.

"What happened to you was not your fault," he said. "You didn't deserve it. I admire you so much for how you've managed to handle what was put on you."

Cassie looked at him. The bitter humor drained from her eyes. There was so much pain in her eyes it broke his heart.

He took a tentative step toward her. "I am proud that my daughter has a mother with so much courage and strength."

Her breath caught as she inhaled. Her lip trembled as she took in the breath. She turned away from him. But she couldn't hide. He saw the tremble skitter across her shoulders.

Xavier didn't want to make her cry again, but if

that was the way to pierce her armor, he'd do it. He had to get through to her. He had to convince her that he was a safe place to land.

"I'm sorry they hurt you. I'm sorry I hurt you. You are a good person, Cassie."

A sob broke through. So quiet, he almost could've imagined it. But he was close enough to taste the salt of her tears in the air between them.

"I just need you to know that I'm here for you, Cassie."

He reached out his hand to her. His index finger was just millimeters away from her shoulder. He almost had her in his grasp when she turned and smacked his hand away.

"I said don't touch me. I don't want your pity."

"It's not pity."

"I don't want any of your smooth talk either. That's what brought me here."

Standing before the woman he loved, the woman he'd lay his life down for, Xavier felt that another explosion had gone off around him. But this time it was right in front of his face. And if he wasn't careful, he'd lose more than another pound of flesh. He'd lose not only his heart but the heart of the woman he loved. Cassie wouldn't die a physical death. But her spirit was on its last breath. He'd need to tread carefully and lightly if he was going to save her soul.

"You look so lovely."

The four women around Cassie all nodded in agreement as they gazed at her reflection in the full-length mirror. Cassie ran her palms down the length of the white dress she wore. It was a simple sundress with a modest bodice that hinted at her cleavage, a ruched waist, and a flaring skirt that ended just below her knees.

Sarai, the former model of the bunch, had given it to her. She was down on her knees with needle and thread making the final alterations so that the dress fit Cassie like a glove. Eva, the scholar of the group, had done Cassie's hair up in a loose bun with wisps hanging to frame her face. Ruhi, the nurse, and Maggie, the vet, had been on the floor playing with Alex, but now joined everyone in the mirror.

"Don't you think your mother looks so pretty?" said Ruhi. She had Alex on her hip. Alex lifted her hand and waved at her mother.

Cassie wiggled her fingers back at her daughter. She still marveled that her daughter was comfortable with every single person on this ranch. For the three years of her life, Alex had not wanted to be held by anyone but Cassie, making daycare an issue. But she happily went into the arms of every resident here at the Purple Heart Ranch, including the brawny soldiers whom Xavier called his true brothers.

"Can you say pretty?" Ruhi sing-songed to Alex. Alex simply grinned at the soon-to-be mother. It was evident that Ruhi was practicing for her own child, but this was a milestone that Alex might not ever be ready for.

"She doesn't respond," said Cassie.

"No," smiled Ruhi, entirely undaunted. "But she understands. She'll talk when she's ready. Won't you, Alex?"

Alex bobbed her head as though she did understand. But her focus was on Ruhi's bright and colorful jewelry.

"And when she does start talking," said Eva, "you'll wish she'd be quiet again."

Eva looked over to her little sister who sat quietly in the corner. Rosalee was playing with Cassie's bouquet, arranging and rearranging the wildflowers in the gathered bunch. The young girl looked up and frowned at her older sister. The women gathered all giggled, but not Cassie.

Cassie didn't appreciate the joke. These women didn't know what it was like to have a special needs child. To wonder if the fault in the child was a result of something that happened in the pregnancy or something that didn't happen. Cassie lay awake many a night looking down at her daughter wondering what she'd done wrong to leave Alex ill-equipped to face the world.

"Rosalee was a preemie," said Eva coming to stand beside Cassie. "She had to stay in the hospital a few weeks before they let our parents bring her home. But look at her now."

Cassie did. She looked at the healthy, bright, spirited little girl. She would've never been able to tell that the child had a rough start in life.

Eva gave Cassie a squeeze. "Alex is beautiful and perfect. I'm so excited that she's a part of our family now. And you as well."

Cassie tried not to stiffen in the woman's embrace, but it was a losing battle. She'd gone without any affection for so long she couldn't remember the simple mechanics of a hug. Cassie was sure Eva caught her discomfort with the display of affection, but she didn't mention it. She simply released Cassie and gave her back her personal space.

Cassie let out a sigh of relief. But at the tail end of the sigh was a breath of remorse. Cassie had always wanted close friendships. Her parents had only allowed her to socialize within the church, and when they'd cut ties with her, not a single one of the friends she thought she had even reached out to her. She didn't want a repeat of that pain. It would be best if she maintained her distance from these women.

"Alex wasn't a preemie," Cassie said. "They think she has Autism, but a highly functional form of the disorder. We won't know for sure until she's older."

"The medical field still doesn't know what causes Autism," said Ruhi. "It could be genetics. It could be environmental."

"So either something in my DNA or something in the place I was living?" Cassie couldn't help it. Her hackles rose. She held out her hands for Alex.

Ruhi passed the child back to her mother. Her face was a mask of compassion as she regarded Cassie. "There's so much we don't understand about the miracle of life. This wasn't your fault, Cassie. I was still drinking wine and alcohol a month before I knew I was pregnant."

Ruhi put her hands over her belly, caressing her hump as though she were rubbing her child's back. Cassie had done neither of those things ever. But she remembered being pregnant and alone and out on the streets.

Alex wiggled until her mother set her down. The little girl made her way back over to Ruhi and climbed onto her lap. Children didn't know how to cast blame or hold grudges. It was a lesson Cassie needed to learn.

Cassie wanted to apologize for her outburst, but she couldn't make her mouth form the words. These women had shown her nothing but kindness in the two days she'd been on the ranch. But Cassie couldn't help her fear that the kindness would be yanked away from her at any moment.

At that moment, a door was yanked open. A tall man with dark skin stood in the doorway blocking out the sun.

"Shut the door, Sean," said Maggie. "Xavier can't see her before the wedding. It's bad luck."

If only they knew how much bad luck was between Cassie and Xavier. The open doorway was the least of their problems.

Sean came in and closed the door behind him. He made a beeline for Ruhi and planted a kiss on the bridge of her nose. Alex, who was still on Ruhi's lap, reached up and touched the jagged scar on his cheek.

"I'm so sorry," said Cassie.

Sean glanced over at her and smiled. When he did, the scar seemed to melt away. What was left was a very handsome man.

"I don't mind," he said. "I'm just happy she got your looks instead of her father's."

A smile jerked the edge of Cassie's lips.

She tugged her lower lip into her mouth to tuck the smile away. Sean straightened from his wife and made his way over to Cassie. "Xavier wanted me to give you this."

Cassie took the box from the man's hand. She opened the lid and gasped. Inside was an exact replica of the ring Xavier had given her four years ago.

Despite her sense of betrayal, Cassie had held

onto the ring for the first two years. She'd worn it on her left hand throughout her pregnancy. But by the second year, she'd realized Xavier was never coming for her, and she put the ring away. It had been stolen at some point during her days moving from shelter to shelter.

"You're exactly as I pictured you," Sean said.

Cassie felt an irrational urge to run and hide under his gaze. What had Xavier said about her to his fellow soldiers?

"You're far more beautiful a woman than I thought he could ever get. And you're way too good for him. Just give me a signal if you want to make a run for it."

Cassie couldn't hide the second grin he'd elicited from her. She read sincerity in his hazel eyes. A man with such a brutal scar would've known adversity. He might understand what she'd been through. Perhaps she could have one friendship on this ranch after all? But the other women shooed Sean out of the room.

"These men," said Maggie. "I'm so glad you're here, Cassie. We finally outnumber them."

"Now we can enact our master plan," said Sarai.

"Which is?" asked Cassie, genuinely curious.

"To turn the barn into a she-shed," said Eva. "Arts and crafts everywhere."

"And we'll watch romantic comedies on movie night," said Maggie.

The women giggled at their dastardly plan. Cassie looked around. Despite herself, the grin that Sean had born spread a bit more across her face at the sisterhood she found herself surrounded by.

"My dad says you have a beautiful voice," said Ruhi. "I hope you'll join the church choir."

"Oh, that would be amazing," said Eva. "That is if you decide you like our church."

"Of course she will," said Maggie. "And she'll be just in time for the church picnic tomorrow."

Cassie hadn't been a part of a church community in years. She hadn't felt welcome in the Lord's House with a baby in her arms but no ring on her finger. Could she really go back to church now, after all these years? She might find a welcoming community there if she came with a ring on her finger.

"That is if you feel up to after your wedding night?" Maggie was saying.

Maggie waggled her eyebrows eliciting another round of giggles from the women gathered. Alex clapped her hands at the joyous laughter spreading around the room. Rosalee rolled her eyes and made her final arrangements to Cassie's bouquet before handing it to her.

Cassie felt heat on her cheeks. Her wedding night would be nothing like these women's first night with their husbands. She'd demanded a purely platonic arrangement. She didn't even want to be Xavier's friend in this relationship. Didn't she?

"Oh, this brings back memories of my wedding," said Ruhi.

"It should," said Maggie. "You only got married two weeks ago."

Cassie couldn't help but do a double take at the woman's belly bump. Two weeks ago? Ruhi had to be a couple months pregnant if she was showing.

Ruhi caught her stare and laughed. "Oh yeah, it was a shotgun wedding. Even more scandalous …" She leaned forward and stage-whispered. "It's not Sean's baby."

"And … he knows?" said Cassie.

"Of course," Ruhi chuckled. "He suggested we get married after my boyfriend dumped me. Michael, that's my ex, he's not ready to be a father. But Sean wanted both me and my baby."

"So that he could stay on the ranch because of the zoning?" asked Cassie.

"Don't believe the zoning line that these guys

feed you," said Sarai. "None of these men do anything they don't want to do. And that includes Xavier."

"Since I've known him," said Maggie, "he's said he would never get married. He never said why though. You're back in his life for a couple of hours before he proposes ..."

She let the sentence linger.

"He could've moved down the street," said Eva. "He could've driven here every day. I don't think it's about the ranch. He's marrying you because he wants to."

The women sighed at the thought. What they didn't understand was the possibility of Xavier choosing her was even scarier than him being obligated to marry her. Love was fickle. Just because it came to town one day didn't mean it would stay forever.

CHAPTER TEN

Xavier walked up to the gazebo. Just two months ago they'd decorated it for Dylan and Maggie's wedding. The decorations hadn't come down because Fran and Eva had used this spot next for their vows. Followed by Reed and Sarai. The decorations had gotten an Indian-Southern Baptist makeover when Sean and Ruhi had taken center stage a couple of weeks ago.

The only addition Xavier made for his nuptials with Cassie was to add a record player and speakers at the back of the gazebo.

"Never thought I'd see you standing here," said Dylan.

"Never thought I'd get her back," he said.

But he had gotten her back. Physically, if not

spiritually. Xavier knew Cassie still didn't trust him. But after they said their vows, he'd have a lifetime to prove to her that he would never leave her again. He'd make her see that he'd meant every one of the vows he'd promised her four years ago. And now he had new ones to tack on that he'd hold fast to every day of their lives.

In the distance, he saw the girls begin their promenade toward them. He made out Cassie immediately. Not simply because she was dressed in white. Because she was a beacon. He'd always find her.

As his gaze focused in on her, he was transported back to that moment five years ago when he'd seen her walking down the street. The sun had lighted on her shoulders, surrounding her with an angelic glow that warmed him from afar. He'd followed her then. She was coming to him now.

Back then, she'd turned to him with a small smile on her face. Now, she gazed up at him with a blank expression. Her features were set not in joy but in duty.

He knew that the main reason she'd agreed to this arrangement was for Alex. Her sense of duty to their child overruled her lack of feelings for him. Her distrust of him because she still believed that he'd abandoned her, misled her, and never came back for her.

Xavier cursed himself for not looking harder for her. For simply taking the word of her parents and not pressing to find out for himself if she had married someone else. To at least seek her out and have a conversation with her to ensure that he wasn't her choice.

He would never doubt again. He would never have to. In just a few minutes, she would be his forever.

Fran placed the needle on the record, and the crooning sounds of Evangeline Taylor filled the early afternoon air. It was the song playing on their many drives through the countryside. The song playing the night he'd promised her forever. It was a gamble to play it now, but the words the singer crooned were as true today as they were all those years ago. The love he had for Cassie was eternal.

From the distance, Xavier saw the light of recognition in Cassie's eyes. Cassie's steps faltered. Luckily, the other women were there by her side. Maggie put a hand to Cassie's back. Eva put one to her shoulder.

Cassie nodded at them. She took a breath and continued down the aisle by herself. She was walking not only toward him, but she was also walking into the family on this ranch. Every one of these people would have her back from this day forward. No one would ever turn her away or turn away from her.

Rosalee held Alex's hands as they walked down the aisle ahead of Cassie. The girls distributed flowers they'd picked from the gardens on the ground as they went. Halfway down the aisle, Alex gave up the flowers and made a beeline for her dad.

Xavier held out his arms and scooped up his little girl. He'd only known her for two days, but he couldn't imagine his life without her. He gave Alex a kiss and then they both turned to her mom.

Cassie's steps were slow and unsteady at first. But she put her shoulders back and kept going. He watched her chest heave as she took deep breaths. He wanted to go to her, but even more, he needed her to come to him. And pretty soon, she was standing before him.

"We are gathered here today to join this man and this woman," Dr. Patel began.

Xavier was already joined with Cassie. Even though they'd been apart for years, the connection to her had never left him. He felt the bond down deep in his spirit. Today, that link would become official.

"The heart is an exceptional organ," Dr. Patel continued. "It can fill to the brim with love. Just when you think it cannot fill anymore, it floods with more love. But just as it can overflow with love, it can break open with hurt and sorrow. A broken heart heals and is almost immediately ready to allow more love in. Until it breaks again. What it takes most people a lifetime to learn is that after each break the task is not to close up the heart, but to leave it open and never let it close again."

Xavier could see Cassie's shoulders tremble as the older man spoke. She hadn't met his gaze. Her eyes were glued downward. She was focusing on the ring on her finger, the exact replica of the one he'd given her four years ago.

He ached to reach out to her and let her know that she would never have to take that ring off again. That he would have her back from this day on. But he knew she wouldn't yet accept his touch. Not yet.

"Xavier has prepared his own vows. Will you join hands to receive them?"

With Alex in one arm, Xavier reached out for Cassie with his free hand. He saw her fingers clench and unclench, only to clinch again. But then she moved her bouquet to one hand and gave him her free one.

Had her hands always been that small? He knew her fingertips hadn't been this rough when they were younger. He added to his vows that she would never have to lift another finger if she didn't want to. He would give her all his sustenance, his support, his strength from this day forward.

"Cassie," Xavier began. "You were my guide to love. I heard your voice, and it opened my heart. It was your light that led me and kept me steady when I was in the darkness. You are my rose garden in a junkyard. You grew inside my heart in a place where love was never meant to exist. You took root and made something beautiful. I promise to tend to you and nourish you and sing to you. That is what I know helps flowers grow, and you are the most beautiful blossom I've ever witnessed. You've had my undying devotion for years, and now, like a weed, you're not getting rid of me."

There was some giggling and chuckling from the audience. Dr. Patel smiled wide. Alex rested her head beneath his chin and placed her hand on his heart.

Cassie's eyes were near to overflowing with tears. She opened her mouth and then shut it. She shut her eyes tight, but the tears streamed down. She glanced from Xavier to Alex, and then down again. She shook her head and pulled her hand away from his.

"I'm sorry," she said. "I can't."

She turned from him and walked down the aisle from where she'd come.

CHAPTER ELEVEN

Cassie was living in a dream. It was the dream she had every night when she closed her eyes, and Xavier was there. He'd hold her close and tell her everything would be all right.

And then in the morning, she'd wake up. She'd wake up to the loneliness and heartache and stress and disappointment of the real world. She'd curse the dream and dread going back to sleep every night, only to curl up into the dream world again and face the cycle of waking disappointment.

But she was awake now.

She stood there with everyone's eyes on her, and all she could do was wait for that horrible moment when she was wrenched from sleep.

But the sun was shining in her face, and her eyes were wide open.

She was awake, and Xavier was making these promises to her. He was far more poetic in reality than in her dreams. Of course, he was. This was the real Xavier. He'd always had that gift of gab along with that charming personality. It would be so easy to believe the words coming out of his mouth.

But she couldn't.

Even if this was reality, she knew it wouldn't last. It couldn't. She'd been down this road and had the tire marks on her heart to prove it.

Reality had come to a dream world. Her mind couldn't wrap around it. So, she ran away.

The sounds of gasps drowned out the music playing on the record player. A few of the women who'd stood at her side a moment ago rose as she passed by. But just as soon as they stood, they each sat back down.

Of course, they did. She wasn't their family. She'd just rejected her way into their group.

The last person she saw was Sean. But he grimaced and rubbed at his shoulder. Ruhi gave him a whack as she glared at him.

He turned to her. "I swear I didn't give any signal."

It was for the best. If they weren't going to stick by her without Xavier, then they never would have stuck by her in her everyday life. It was just another heartache she'd avoid. She didn't need to be abandoned by anyone else. She'd reached her quota years ago.

And so she ran.

But she hadn't gotten too far. She didn't know where she was going. Cassie stopped running and looked up at the sky. God was only supposed to give you what you could handle. Why was He constantly putting more on her plate then?

Her heart pounded and ached. She just needed a few minutes to herself to settle down and get it under control. She spied salvation at a pier overlooking a small pond.

She walked over the wooden planks, her heels clicking as she avoided the holes between each board. Cassie sat down. She dangled her feet over the edge, making sure not to get her dress dirty. It was a loaner, and she planned to return it to Sarai in the same condition she'd been given it.

She caught her breath. But, still, her heart pounded. So robust, so loud, she was certain it was coming out of her chest.

Cassie was so focused on the pounding of her

heart that she hadn't heard the footsteps coming up behind her. Xavier lowered himself down to a sitting position on the pier. His legs were so long that the tips of his shoes tapped the surface of the water causing a ripple to break the smooth lines and disrupt the peaceful water.

He said nothing. He also sat at the farthest part of the pier, not encroaching on her space. When they were younger, he'd press boundaries with her. Always getting a little closer, kissing a little longer. But the man he'd become, this man, hadn't rushed in.

"I can't," she said.

He nodded, looking out across the water. "Okay."

And that was it. No cajoling, no smooth talking. Just simple agreement.

Cassie's heart pounded louder in her ears. Shouldn't she feel relieved? Instead, she felt even more bereft.

"We'll have to move off the ranch in two weeks," he said.

Right. The ranch. That's what this was all about. That was his only concern, not her.

"I had only been looking at one bedroom apartments, but I'm sure I can find a small house to rent in a couple of weeks. It won't be much on what I get monthly from the Army. But it will be better than that place you called home."

"House?"

He turned to face her now. "Yes. A house. For the three of us."

"Us?"

Xavier's gray eyes made a slow trek across the features of her face before returning to gaze directly into her eyes, his own features stern with resolve. "Marriage was an option. Breaking up our family is not. I understand if you don't want to be my wife. But we're life partners, forever. You and Alex are my responsibility. If later, you decide you want to marry someone else ... we'll figure it out."

He'd turned from her during that brief pause in his statement. When he spoke of marrying someone else, the stiff posture of his back slumped, caving inward. His carefully blank features darkened with despair when he said they'd figure it out.

But Cassie didn't want to marry anyone else. Those vows she'd spoken years ago had imprinted on her heart and closed it off to anyone else. With the words Xavier had spoken today during their brief and ill-fated ceremony, he'd wrenched the doors open.

With her heart open, Cassie saw what could've

been if he'd come back in time. Maybe they could've been a family? Maybe they could've been a couple, a true husband and a wife?

But she was also reminded of what did happen when none of those dreams had come true. The pain. The hurt. It was all waiting there, ready to pounce again if she left her heart open. That's why she had to close it. To protect herself.

"I can't change the past," Xavier said. "Neither of us can. We'll drive ourselves crazy thinking what could've been. I can only give you right now and promise the future."

He turned to face her. Cassie tried to block out the earnestness she saw in his eyes. He'd never lied to her when they were together. He made fun, he made things up, he stretched to the truth to get her to laugh. But never a lie.

Every time he'd left and said he would come back, he had. Including the last time. They'd just missed each other.

"I will never leave you again. You will never be alone. You will never be in need."

Inside, Cassie was drained from trying to close the chambers of her heart. A feat that had been easy days ago proved impossible at this moment. Her heart was wide open, and the memories of what love felt like were rising to the surface. She was so full of the memories that tears pooled at the corner of her eye.

Xavier reached out and caught the first teardrop before it could fall. "I promised myself I'd take things slow with you. Give you the room you needed to learn to trust me again. I can still do that. I can wait forever for you. I just need you to know that things have never changed for me, and they never will. You're the only woman I've ever loved. The only woman I want in my life. Since the day I met you, I've done everything in my power to prove myself worthy of you. That's what I'm going to do for the rest of my life."

Cassie looked up at Xavier. The years fell away, and she saw the young man, so full of promise, that she'd fallen in love with. The man who hadn't thought himself worthy of her. The man who'd gone away to better himself so that he could take care of her. In an instant, all the hurt melted away. She felt overwhelmed by the love she felt for him.

She reached up and took Xavier's face in her hands. She wished she could melt his sorrow away just as hers had gone. "You were always worthy of me."

His eyes searched hers. Hope shone in the gray

depths, like a ray of sun peeking out after a cloudy day.

"I'm yours," Cassie said.

Xavier's eyes closed as though he were saying a silent prayer of gratitude.

"Now and forever."

And for the second time in their lives, Cassie and Xavier sealed their vows with a kiss.

CHAPTER TWELVE

Xavier didn't let go of Cassie's hand as they walked away from the gazebo to the reception. The barn doors were thrown wide open with the sweet smell of barbecue already mixing with the earthy smell of the hay surrounding the structure. Picnic tables were set up both inside and out of the barn which housed the guy's gaming consoles. Though Xavier noticed there was now a supply cabinet taken over with arts and crafts supplies in the corner that hadn't been there before.

The art supplies couldn't hold his attention. The woman on his arm captured his every waking thought. When Xavier and Cassie had returned from the pier, hand in hand, they'd skipped the rest of the ceremony, having already renewed their vows over the water before the eyes of God. They'd picked up pens and signed the marriage certificate before their friends instead.

Spoken promises were one thing. This time, Xavier was determined to make this deal a legal and binding contract that no man, woman, or parent would put asunder. And he'd done that. Mrs. Cassandra Ramos had his ring, his promise, and his power of attorney. No one and nothing would ever come between them again.

Better yet, this time the occasion had been witnessed by their family. Cassie didn't realize it yet, but she was in a gang that she would never be able to get out of. The residents and workers of the Purple Heart Ranch had a way of collecting people. Once you were in, there was no getting out.

From the speakers inside the barn that they'd faced outwards, the music picked up, but no one danced. Faces screwed at the sounds of the old spirituals that Xavier and his new bride loved. But one by one, everyone began bopping their heads and moving their feet in time to the upbeat gospel music.

Couples twirled on the dance floor. Dogs yipped between feet. Xavier spun Cassie in his arms until the smile that had been so fleeting on her face the past hour spread and then stayed put. She was grinning wide and laughing when he brought her close. Her smile went tentative, like a crack in a fine piece of China where the adhesive glue was still drying.

"You know I used to dream of this," he said, peering down into her navy blue eyes. "Us dancing on our wedding day surrounded by our family and friends."

She tugged at her lower lip before letting it and the words loose. "I dreamed it too."

She looked away when she spoke the words, as though she didn't want him to see the tinge of sadness at the edge of her eyelids. Xavier placed his index finger under her chin and turned her face back to him.

"It's not a dream anymore," he said. "It's our future."

She let out a small sigh as she took a step deeper into his hold, as though she were about to relay a secret that she only wished him to hear. "I hated waking up from that dream. But I also hated going to sleep and dreaming because I knew it wasn't real."

"It is real. This is real."

"I know."

She took another deep breath. With each breath she took and released, he visibly saw the tension leaving her body. Until finally, Xavier felt Cassie relax in his arms. So, he dipped her.

Cassie gasped as her world turned upside down. When Xavier righted her, she blinked rapidly, and then she grinned. Her grin stayed as he pressed her to him, into a hold that she never had to leave.

She slid her hand over his shoulder and squeezed. Then her hand slipped down his back and again squeezed. It was a touch of affection, but it hurt. Xavier couldn't hide the wince. It had been a long time since a non-professional had touched his back. But he would endure the pain if it meant his wife's happiness.

His wife. Cassie was finally his wife in name and in deed. He'd pledged to never let her go, but he did allow Reed to cut in. And then Dylan. Followed by Fran, and finally Sean.

Xavier stood back and watched Cassie loosen and lighten as each of his friends, his brothers, swayed with her and twirled her around. When she was finally returned to his arms by Dr. Patel, she resembled the girl he'd fallen for all those years ago.

Her blue gaze was more an opaque topaz than a dark night at sea. Her cheeks were pink. Her smile was wide.

Xavier was eager to have her all to himself as

soon as possible. He was thinking up ways to make an exit when the music changed to a Top 40's girl power anthem. Maggie and Sarai made a beeline toward Cassie, sweeping her up into their all-girls conga line. The men stood back, grinning ear to ear, as they watched their wives shimmy and wave their hands to a tune that asserted they didn't need no man. But as soon as the song was over, each woman happily returned to the arms of the man they'd pledged to make their lives with.

That included Cassie. She walked slowly toward him. Her careful hairdo now undone. The bright makeup fading from her face under the sun's rays and with the exertion from the nonstop dancing. She was a vision.

But looking past his wife, Xavier saw his perfect opportunity for escape. Curled up under one of the picnic tables he saw his daughter lying on Star's belly. Spin rested his head on Alex's knee, and Soldier kept watch.

When Cassie came into his arms, he pointed. "We should probably put her to bed."

Cassie turned to where he pointed. Her ahhh caused the other women to turn and ahhh as well. Xavier crawled under the table and retrieved his sleeping daughter, but not before everyone whipped out their cellphone cameras to take pictures of the little angel and her fierce protectors. Finally, with his daughter in one arm and his wife on the other, he made his way back to their little cabin on the ranch.

At the threshold, Xavier looked from the sleeping toddler to his wife whom he was supposed to carry over the threshold.

"You wanna take her so I can carry you both over the threshold?"

"Don't be silly." Cassie pushed the door open and entered. "We haven't done anything traditional so far. Why start now?"

They laid Alex on the bed in the room she'd shared with Cassie the other night. The sun was starting to set and cast a soft glow over the interior of the room. In the lighting, Alex truly did resemble a sleeping angel.

"She's so beautiful," Cassie sighed.

"Just like her mother."

"You got your ring on my finger, you don't have to flatter me anymore."

"Yes, I did. I got my ring on your finger. Again. It'll stay there this time."

Looking down at Cassie, Xavier felt breathless. His hands tingled, and he knew the only thing that would stop the sensation was reaching out and bringing his wife into his hold. He reached for her, and she came to him.

Xavier leaned down and pressed his lips to hers. They'd skipped this part at the ceremony, but they made up for it now. He pulled her close telling her with his body that he would never let her go. He deepened the kiss trying to wipe away four years of hurt and anguish. But even as his body was ready to give her more, he pulled back.

"We can wait," he said.

Cassie opened her eyes and blinked at him as though she were waking from a dream. One side of her mouth lifted into a shy grin. "I don't see the need. You just promised yourself to me forever. In the eyes of God, we're married."

Xavier sent up a silent prayer of gratitude. That was exactly the answer he was hoping for. He pulled Cassie back into his embrace, determined that nothing would keep them apart.

"Eggs."

His lips hovered over hers. Just a breath between them when she made her request.

"Eggs?" Xavier asked. "You want eggs?"

"I didn't say that," said Cassie.

They both turned to the bed. Alex sat up, wiping the sleep from her eyes. She looked at them brightly as though she'd slept the night away and was ready for a new day.

"Oh, my gosh!" Cassie shot out of Xavier's arms and rushed over to the bed. "That's her first word. You're hungry, baby? You want eggs?"

"Eggs," Alex said, holding up her arms for Xavier.

"Eggs? You mean Xavier?"

"No, darling," said Xavier, coming over to lean over his little girl. "I'm Daddy."

"Eggs," Alex repeated, frowning this time, opening and closing her hands in the universal language of a toddler that said pick me up.

Xavier chuckled as he picked his daughter up. "All right. Eggs, it is."

CHAPTER THIRTEEN

Cassie was surrounded by warmth. Not heat from a fire or a furnace. It was the type of warmth that came from being snuggled up under covers on a winter's night. It was the type of warmth that came from a cup of tea with just the right amount of honey. It was the type of warmth that came after a kiss was left on the lips.

She had been kissed recently. It had been a brief touch of the lips, but the feeling lingered on into her dream. She knew she was dreaming. She knew she was dreaming of Xavier. But there was no dread in her heart.

Her heart was open in the dream. Open and ready to receive love. His love.

It was Xavier's arms around her. It was Xavier's

kiss at her temple. It was Xavier giving off that warmth. For the first time in years, she hadn't held her breath in the dream. Neither had she dreaded waking up.

She turned her head and looked up at him. He smiled down at her with love in his eyes. He leaned closer and pressed his lips to hers.

Warmth tingled in her fingertips where she grazed the fine hairs of his temple. She felt the stubble of his new day's growth on her chin. She tasted the slight tang of the barbecue they'd had at their reception.

Wow, this was the most vivid, sensory dream she'd ever had.

Then she realized. "I'm not dreaming."

"No. Not unless you're inside my head as well as my heart." Xavier closed his eyes and winced. "Wow, marriage has made me cheesy."

"I liked what you said. It was perfect. Everything is perfect."

She brushed her hand over the stubble on his chin. The dark hair growing there made him look slightly dangerous, and that thrilled her. She'd always known in her heart of hearts that Xavier wasn't a bad guy. He was good to his core, even though he liked to play the bad boy.

Xavier slid his thumb over her cheek. A trail of heat traced his movements. "Everything's good right now, but just wait. I'm going to make it perfect. I promise you will never have to worry about a thing again."

She pressed her forehead against his, hoping that he would hear the truth of her words. "I don't need anything else. I have everything I ever wanted."

She had a home that she would never be kicked out of. She had the man of her dreams holding her in his warm embrace. The only thing remaining that she wanted was to consummate this legal marriage as they'd done their spiritual one.

"Eggs?"

But that would have to wait until they trained their daughter to sleep in her own bed, in her own room.

Cassie looked between her chest and Xavier's. Alex was curled up between them, eyes open and shining bright. That was another thing Cassie was thankful for. She had her daughter who was speaking now.

Alex rubbed the sleep from her eyes. She sat up from her space in between both of her parents. She grinned at her mother, then she held out her arms for her father.

"Eggs."

"It's Daddy," said Xavier, taking his little girl into his arms. "Try it, angel. Dad. Dada."

Alex ignored him and snuggled into his chest. She looked up to her mother and held one arm out to Cassie. Cassie scooted closer so that she was included in the cocoon.

Cassie rested her head on the other side of Xavier's chest and smiled over at her daughter. Alex looked content. Xavier gave a sigh of contentment. Cassie felt their happiness echo in the boundless chambers of her heart.

"Of course you're the one to get her talking," said Cassie, looking up accusingly at her husband. "You always had a way with women."

"There's only one woman I want to have my way with." He waggled his eyebrows.

Cassie blushed. She'd forgotten that side of him, the side that liked to tease and taunt her. In retaliation, she gave him a whack on the back.

Xavier winced. His back bowed as he cradled Alex to his heart.

Cassie sat up in alarm. "Xavier?"

"It's fine." He sat Alex on the floor. The little girl walked away from them and began exploring her father's room. Xavier stood. He tried to smile, but the wince was still there.

"It's not fine," said Cassie. "I'm not that strong. Are you hurt?"

He sighed. "There's something you should know, something I need to show you."

So many things went through Cassie's mind. What she did not expect was for Xavier to unbutton the dress shirt he'd worn on their wedding day. They'd all fallen asleep in their wedding clothes. Cassie was a rumpled mess of white fabric. But she couldn't focus on her state of dress, she was far too taken by her husband's increasing state of undress.

Cassie looked from Xavier's bared chest and the rippling muscles of his abdomen, to her daughter on the floor playing with his shoes, and back to Xavier's finely honed flesh.

"Xavier now is not the time for that."

He gave her a smile that didn't reach his eyes. He balled the shirt up and tossed it on the bed. "I told you I was injured while in the service."

"Yes."

Slowly, he turned. Cassie couldn't hide her gasp. His back was a ruin of dark, angry skin.

"It was a suicide bomber," he said. "In retaliation for information I was able to gain from an informant. People always told me that my mouth would get me in trouble one day. They were right."

Cassie took tentative steps toward him. "Does it hurt?"

"I'm not in constant pain anymore, but it can be uncomfortable in some situations."

Like the discomfort from being slapped on the back. "I'm so sorry. I didn't know."

Cassie folded her hands over her chest. Xavier turned to her. He unballed her fists, putting her fingers on his chest.

"When I thought you had moved on," he said, "I didn't have a care in the world. I took a lot of chances because I didn't think I had anything to live for."

Cassie lowered her head from all the sorrow she felt in her heart. Xavier tilted her head back up, and the tears fell. He wiped them away one by one until she saw him clearly.

"When I was lying there thinking I was going to die," he said, "I heard you sing to me. It was all I could think about; that one day I might hear you sing again. That's what got me to hold on for another day and then another. In the hospital, someone had an Evangeline Taylor CD. I'd listen to it on repeat. It got lost along the way until I found the album in the music shop, and there I found you."

Cassie wrapped her arms around his neck, careful to avoid his back.

"I'm not going to break, Cassie."

"I just don't want to cause you any more pain."

"Having the two of you in my life, I doubt I'll ever feel any pain again." He put his nose into her hair and breathed deeply.

"Ohh, that one was a little on the cheesy-side."

"Wow, I've really turned into a complete cheeseball."

CHAPTER FOURTEEN

Xavier felt on top of the world as he handed his wife out of his truck. Cassie stayed close to him as he lifted Alex from her car seat and kept her in his arms. He had his daughter in one arm and the woman he loved in the other. Life couldn't get any better than this.

He'd parked his old truck between a shiny new Lexus and a fully loaded minivan in the church parking lot. Looking back at the three cars, Xavier wondered if he should invest in a new car, something more fitting for a family man. He was a little tight on funds at the moment.

That was another thing he needed to look into, getting a job. He hadn't needed much living on his own at the ranch. But now that he had a wife and child, they'd both need new clothes. Alex would need toys. And he wanted to cover Cassie in jewelry and new appliances and music and whatever else he could think of.

She'd gone without for far too long. Yesterday was the last day of her living in poverty. He'd put her into the lap of luxury. He just needed to earn a few more coins to do it.

"Hey, Xavier," grinned a woman in a low cut dress that definitely wasn't church picnic appropriate.

"Good morning ..." Xavier couldn't remember her name. He never remembered women's names. They'd always been a momentary distraction for him to help him try to forget, for just a few seconds, what he'd lost in his past.

"Melanie and I saved a seat for you on our blanket."

Melanie was standing beside her unnamed friend in a skirt that was raised high enough to send up its own prayers.

"Thanks," said Xavier, as he draped his arm around Cassie. "But I'll be sharing a blanket with my family."

The two women turned to Cassie. "Oh, is this your sister?"

"No," said Xavier. "This is my wife."

"Wife?" said Melanie. Her mouth fell open, and her gaze went wide. "You're his wife?"

Cassie shrank back. She'd never been one for confrontations. She never liked being out in public where women would gawk at the two of them as though they didn't belong together.

"And the little girl?" said the other woman. "Is she your daughter?"

"Yes, this is my daughter, Alex."

It was the first time Xavier had seen Alex frown. On the ranch, she offered smiles and giggles to every single person. But in the face of these two women, she looked close to tears.

"Oh," said Melanie. "I see."

Xavier knew what the two were thinking. That he'd only married Cassie because he'd knocked her up. Xavier pulled Cassie closer to him and placed a kiss on her temple.

"This is Cassie Ramos, my first and only love. I fell in love with her four years ago, but we were torn apart. I haven't been the same man since. I finally found her again just a few days ago, and I put a ring on her finger as soon as I could. No, she'll never get away from me again."

And with that, he moved his family forward and left the two women gaping after them.

"You didn't have to say all those things," said Cassie.

He looked down at her. Her navy blue eyes were as clear as a sparkling gem as she regarded him. There was a small hint of something that looked like pride at the corners of her eyes. The sight made Xavier feel ten times taller.

"Why not?" He pressed a kiss to her forehead. "It's true. You are the love of my life."

She grinned as she nuzzled into the space beneath his chin. "But you don't have to put on a show every time one of your exes comes over."

"I don't have any exes," he said. "Not since you."

They stopped in a clearing. To their right, Dylan and Maggie had already set up their blanket, and the dogs were all sitting obediently waiting for Maggie to deliver treats. Alex shot out of her father's arms and made a beeline for the dogs. When the dogs saw Alex, they forgot their obedience, stood and wagged their tails as the little girl came in their midst.

Xavier turned back to Cassie. He noted she stared at him with an unreadable expression on her face. He pulled out their blanket and spread it wide, before taking her hand and tugging her down with him.

"Cassie, there's been no one in my life since the day I met you. I flirt a lot, yes. I seek out attention, but that's where it ends. I haven't even kissed another woman in the last four years. It just didn't feel right. No one was you."

She took in a slow, deep breath before she met his gaze. "Me neither."

"And now you're all mine again. Now and forever."

Xavier leaned down and kissed his wife, his one and only love. He'd only meant for the kiss to be a pressed promise to her lips. But the moment he tasted her sweetness, he lost himself and deepened the kiss, searching for more of the taste he'd lost and now found.

"Get a room, you two."

If they hadn't been on holy ground, surrounded by families and children, Xavier would've given Reed a lewd gesture. Instead, he made a face at his brother who'd set up a blanket on the other side of them.

Xavier sat back on the blanket and watched Alex run circles around Maggie's dogs. A few other children came over and tentatively approached the dogs. Xavier looked at the kids in their fine clothes while Alex's clothes were rough around the edges. He'd need to take his daughter shopping soon. She would have the best of everything.

He ran his hand up and down Cassie's shirtsleeve. A thread came loose. He'd have to do the same for his wife.

"What's that look on your face?" Cassie asked.

"Just plotting how I'm going to give you the world."

"You and Alex are my world."

He grinned back at her as his heart swelled. How had he lived the last four years without her smile? The memory of it was a pale comparison to the real thing.

He leaned in and pressed another kiss to the corner of her lip. He held his breath this time. Otherwise, he'd surely spend the entire picnic making a meal of his wife.

The sounds of music filled the air. Cassie turned to the makeshift stage, that was really just a patch of concrete at the back of the church. The choir began a rendition of an old gospel song that was on their favorite Evangeline Taylor album. Cassie closed her eyes and swayed her head to the music.

"Sing it for me," said Xavier.

She opened her eyes. She tugged at her bottom

lip, hesitating for only a second. Then, looking at only him, she began to sing.

This was the voice that had called him out of the agony of the bomb on that fateful day. This was the voice that pushed him to open his eyes and greet a new day every morning. This was the voice that he kept in his heart and held tight. Now, it was out of its cage and singing loudly for everyone to hear.

As Cassie hit the higher notes, Xavier realized the music had stopped. So had the singing choir. The only thing that could be heard was Cassie's voice.

Cassie's gaze was still on him. She didn't see that everyone in the entire congregation had stopped what they were doing. They were all now staring at her in delight and amazement.

When she hit the final note, she smiled at him. But a second later she realized the deafening silence. Her smile fell, and she turned and saw. Embarrassment covered her cheeks.

"Cassie, that was beautiful," said Ruhi, coming forward from the ranks of the choir. "Please, come and sing with us."

"I ..." Cassie began, looking between Ruhi, the crowd, and back to Xavier.

Before Cassie could demur, Xavier rose. He

brought his wife to stand alongside him. He guided her to the front of the crowd, onto the concrete stage with the other singers. He placed her front and center in between Ruhi and Maggie and then stepped back.

Cassie's eyes pleaded with him. But Maggie took one of her hands, Ruhi took the other. She turned to the women who smiled encouragingly at her.

The choir began another familiar tune. Cassie took a deep breath. After a second, she joined her voice with theirs. Cassie's voice trilled overtop of every other singer, like an angel flitting by over the tops of the heads of mere mortals. No one in the congregation spoke, no one moved. All eyes were rapt on Cassie as her voice rose stronger.

When the song came to an end, there was silence. Then, a beat later, the backyard of the church was filled with thunderous applause. Maggie and Ruhi embraced a pink-cheeked Cassie.

Another tune began. This time a call and response song that had all of the congregation joining in. Xavier opened his mouth to join in when someone tapped him on the shoulder.

"Specialist Ramos?"

Xavier turned and faced a man who was just as big and broad as he was. The man sported a cropped haircut favored by those in the military, but he wore no uniform. Likely ex-military. And then recognition dawned.

"Mason Jones? Of Strategic Maneuvers Contractors?"

Mr. Jones stuck out his hand, and Xavier took it.

"Are you a member of this church?" asked Xavier.

"I do some work with Dr. Patel," said Mr. Jones. "He's a great man, does a lot for the soldiers returning to civilian life."

On that, Xavier had to agree. He would not have adjusted well to everyday life without his sessions with Dr. Patel.

"I was going to call you next week," said Mr. Jones, "but it's good that I saw you here. There's a spot that's opened up with my company. We need a communications expert in Yemen."

Xavier looked down at Alex who ran around his legs followed by Star and the rest of the dog pack.

Mr. Jones stepped out of the way of the ragtag bunch, a smile on his face as he did so. He faced Xavier before continuing on with the details of the job. "It's out of the combat zone, which should work now that I see you have a family. But it is a three-month contract."

It was a sweet deal. Three months was hardly any time when deployment could last half a year or longer. And he'd be safe, out of combat.

Xavier had already seen the pay scale for this type of contract work. He'd be able to give Cassie and Alex more, the clothes they needed, a speech therapist for Alex, all the toys she could ever dream of, maybe an addition to the house for more children because he knew he wanted more children with Cassie and soon.

"Think about it," said Mr. Jones, "and let me know."

CHAPTER FIFTEEN

"You have to join the choir," said Ruhi.

"Oh, yes, you must," Maggie piped, reciting the same tune. "We'd love to have you."

All around the two girls, Cassie saw other choir members bob their heads as though they were harmonizing a new chorus. Out in the gathered crowd, many people had risen from their picnic blankets and were still applauding the performance. Cassie waited for the urge to duck her head at the praise to come over her.

It didn't.

She'd always been modest about her singing talents. But the appreciation she felt from this crowd made warmth spread all throughout her chest. For the first time in a long time, Cassie wanted to join in and not shy away from the crowd.

"Sarai can't hold a tune," Ruhi continued. "And Eva has study group a lot right now since she's getting close to midterms."

"Plus your voice is out of this world," said Maggie Her brown eyes sparkled brightly with excitement. She even panted a bit like one of her dogs. "We need you."

It had been so long since Cassie had joined her voice to others in praise. It had been a long time since she'd lifted her voice in praise to the Lord. She and the Savior hadn't been on speaking terms for a while.

But now, for the first time in years, Cassie sent up a prayer of gratitude. She had so much to be thankful for. In just a couple of days, her life had changed drastically.

She'd lost her job and gained the position she'd always wanted for herself; that of homemaker. She'd lost her housing and found the home of her dreams. But most importantly, she'd found the love of her life and opened her heart again.

God was smiling at her. He probably always had been. It had been Cassie who had closed her heart and turned away from His light.

Now that her heart was once again open, she looked up to see herself surrounded by a community eager to embrace her. She had a home, security, and something she never thought she'd ever had back in her life again. Love was back in her life.

The chambers of her heart opened even wider until Cassie was certain she'd burst. It was scary to be this open. She felt vulnerable, as though something unwanted could slip inside. But even though she was wide open and exposed, she felt protected.

"I think she should be a soloist," Maggie was saying.

Dylan came up from behind and gave Cassie a nudge with his shoulder. "Don't let these two talk you into something you don't want to do."

"Says the man who talked me into marrying him less than an hour after meeting him," said Maggie.

Dylan wrapped his wife up in his arms and planted a kiss on her forehead. "Smartest thing I ever did."

"Just give me the signal, and I'll get you out of here," Sean stage-whispered in Maggie's ear.

Ruhi waggled a finger at the man. "Don't get me started on you, buddy."

Sean caught his wife's finger and proceeded to plant a kiss in the palm of her hand.

Cassie smiled at the two couples. She didn't give any signals. She didn't want to push these women away. She didn't want to push anyone away. She felt warm and welcomed, and she wanted to keep herself fully immersed in the feeling.

Cassie saw Alex running around Reed and Sarai's picnic blanket. Alex had the hugest grin on her face as she chased the dogs and was chased by the dogs. The only thing missing from the picture was her husband. And then she saw him.

Xavier's back was to her. The fabric stretched smooth across the planes of his back. No one would be able to tell that there were scars there. They were scars that only she saw, only she touched.

He'd promised to take care of her, to have her back. And she would do the same for him. This was the first day of the rest of their lives.

She's spent so long being apart from him that the short distance seemed like a vast desert. She wanted to be by his side, standing before him, standing behind him every second of the day. Cassie excused herself from her new family of friends, with promises to come to the next choir practice, and made her way over to her husband.

As Cassie got closer, she noticed Xavier was talking to a man. He wore no uniform, but something about his stature read that he'd spent time in the military.

"We need a communications expert in Yemen."

From the back, Cassie saw Xavier nod his head as though in agreement. She knew that that was Xavier's job in the military. She supposed this man was looking for recommendations for an expert overseas.

"It's out of the combat zone, which should work now that I see you have a family. But it is a three-month contract."

Wait? His family? Three months?

But surely they weren't talking about Xavier going overseas. He'd just promised Cassie he'd never leave her again. She had to have missed a part of the conversation. So why was Xavier shaking the man's hand as though he was sealing a deal?

"Think about it, and let me know. The job pays well, better than an army salary. You're our first pick."

"Thank you for considering me." Xavier stuck out his hand. "I'll give you a call in a couple of days."

Cassie heard a crashing sound. It filled up her ears until they were ringing. It punched at her heart until she was certain a hole was in her chest. She felt the chambers of her heart clench as they shook.

Xavier whirled around, eyes wide as though he sensed danger. His gaze met hers. There was concern etched on his face as he looked down at her. Off in the distance, Cassie heard an animal cry out in pain.

"Cassie? Sweetheart, what's wrong?"

She was in his arms, but her limbs felt numb. That cry had come from her. She could barely make out her own voice as she spoke. "You're leaving?"

Xavier's hold tightened on her. His face was still a muddle of confusion.

"You're leaving me. You're leaving us."

The fog cleared from his gray eyes as comprehension dawned, and he sighed. But more importantly, he didn't deny it. Cassie turned to go, to get away from there. But his arms clamped around her.

CHAPTER SIXTEEN

The sound of Cassie's cry of pain sent Xavier into a panic. The sight of her shoulders caving in and her face contorting and then that godawful sound coming from her hit him in his gut.

He thought the worst day of his life had been when he'd come back to find her gone, married to someone else. That pain was topped by finding her and his daughter living in squalor. Seeing her in pain, because she thought he was abandoning her, gutted him.

When she tried to leave, he caught her in his arms and held. "Cassie, honey, I'm not leaving you."

She shoved at his arm, trying to break free of him. "You're going overseas, back to war."

Xavier grasped both of her shoulders tightly in his hands. "For a job, to get money to provide for us."

But still, she turned to and fro, desperate to get out of his hold. Her head tilted away from him. Her eyes closed as though she couldn't even stand to look at him. Tears pricked the edges of her eyelids.

All around them, people were starting to stare. Xavier was used to being the center of attention. But he knew Cassie hated it. She much preferred to add her unique voice to a chorus than to be singled out.

Too bad for her. She needed to be set straight on this point, and it didn't matter to Xavier if everyone knew this fact.

"Cassie, I want to give you everything you deserve, a better life."

That stopped her flailing. She stilled, opening her eyes and peering at him. She took deep, heaving breaths of air that he worried she might be hyperventilating.

"I never wanted any of that," she hissed. Her next words came out on a sob. "All I ever wanted was you. But you can't stand being with me for long. You keep leaving."

Xavier brought her into his embrace, tucking her head beneath his chin and wrapping his arms around her thin shoulders. God, she was so thin.

She'd gone without for so long because of him. He couldn't let that continue. He needed to put food on the table, new clothes on her back, give her a bigger house. This job would provide that. He just needed to make her see.

"It's just a few months," he began.

She shook her head and started backing away again. "You said that the last time."

She was right. He had said that the last time they'd seen each other. But he'd come back. Every time he'd come back for her. This would be no different.

"Cass—" He reached for her, but she jerked away from him. "It's my job to take care of you. This is my only skill."

"No. It's leaving; that's your only skill. I'm not waiting anymore. I should've known better than to let you into my heart again."

She continued backing away from him. Her blue eyes turned cold. Her jawline went hard. With each step she took away from him, Xavier felt shards piercing his heart.

"I'm the one leaving this time," she said. "I'm taking Alex and going."

"Cassie, you are not leaving."

"Why not? You do it all the time. We're not

staying so you can leave over and over again. That's worse than being abandoned."

She turned away from him then. Tiny explosions were going off behind his eyes as he watched the love of his life, his reason for staying alive, walk away from him. Was this what she'd felt when she'd thought he'd left her?

It was worse than the peeling of the skin from his burns. He felt his soul was being excised from his body. Xavier felt as though all was lost. And then Cassie whirled around and faced him, and things got worse than he'd ever imagined.

"Where's Alex?"

It took Xavier a second to tear his gaze away from his wife and focus on his daughter. But Alex was not on the blanket. He looked to the neighboring blankets where the other ranch inhabitants had set up. But they had all dispersed, and Alex wasn't on any of those blankets either.

"You were supposed to be watching her," Cassie accused, her voice going shrill.

"Don't worry." Xavier was certain one of his friends had his daughter. "We'll find her."

CHAPTER SEVENTEEN

All eyes were on them as they argued. Well, Cassie argued and shouted at her husband making a spectacle. She'd had gazes on her and whispers around her when her pregnancy began to show. The shame and solitude had cloaked her then. So much so that she had willingly climbed into the backseat of her father's station wagon when he'd wanted to send her away.

Now, she didn't care about the eyes on her. Shame and shunning were the furthest things from her mind. All she cared about was finding her daughter.

"She was playing on the blanket," said Sarai.

"Then she was with the dogs," said Maggie.

They'd found all the members of the ranch and

Alex wasn't with any of them. Cassie felt bile rise from the pit of her stomach. She wanted to turn an accusing eye on Xavier, but she couldn't lift her head from the support of his chest. If he hadn't been there to lean on, she'd certainly collapsed to the ground.

"She's here," he insisted as he leaned down to her ear. He gave her a squeeze and didn't let go.

The members of the ranch began turning here and there, shouting Alex's name.

"She's nonverbal," Cassie said, but her voice didn't carry far over the shouting. "She won't respond."

It's why Cassie never took her eyes off her daughter. Until these past couple of days. Because she'd let her guard down after the wedding. She'd opened her heart. She'd gotten hurt again. And now her daughter was lost.

"Don't worry," said someone. Maybe Eva? Cassie was too out of her mind with worry to determine. "She couldn't have gotten far. No one in the congregation would let her come to any harm."

But Cassie didn't know these people. They didn't care about her. Except they'd all stopped what they were doing and began searching the grounds for Alex.

"All right, everyone, listen up." Xavier's voice

broke through Cassie's fog. His arms tightened around her even more as he spoke. "We're looking for a little girl. Gray eyes, black hair. She was in a blue dress. Her name is Alex, but she won't respond, so we have to look everywhere. We'll break into groups and search."

A calm settled over Cassie as she watched Xavier take charge. Though she was still shaken, she had every confidence that he'd find Alex and bring her back into her arms, safe and sound. When he did find Alex and put her daughter back in her arms, Cassie wanted to go back into Xavier's arms.

She wanted to go back to sitting on a picnic blanket in his loose embrace. She wanted to go back to how she'd woken up this morning lying next to him. She wanted to come right back to this moment of leaning on him for his love and support.

Try as she might, Cassie couldn't get the chambers of her heart to close again. They were wide open and giving gratitude and thanks to the people searching for Alex. But mostly, the chambers would close because it was so filled with love for the man who held her in his arms.

The girls from the ranch were at her back. Their husbands were fanning out leading the search party. The community was looking out. And Fran was at the helm, leading the search while holding her close.

From the safety of his arms, Cassie knew that no matter how hard she tried, she'd never be able to shut him out. Even through all these years, he'd never left her heart. And she knew she'd never left his. No matter where he went, he'd always be with her. Even if that was to Yemen or anywhere in the world.

He might leave for a time, but he'd always find his way back to her. They'd always find their way back together. Just like they'd find Alex.

"We'll find her," he promised now.

And Cassie believed him. "Last I saw her, she was with the dogs."

"Wait," said Xavier. "Where are the dogs?"

CHAPTER EIGHTEEN

Xavier held Cassie's hand tightly in his. He believed with every fiber in his being that they'd find Alex. Still, his heart pounded each second he didn't know where his little girl was, what she was doing, if she needed him.

How had he considered leaving for months and not seeing his baby girl, not holding Cassie? He felt sucker punched at the thought of it now. Not just because Alex was outside of his reach. He felt gutted because, after all these years, he finally had Cassie back within his arms, and he was not ready to put even a mile of space between them.

It was out of the question. He couldn't leave his family behind. He couldn't take them with him. His only option was to stay.

He'd stay and find another way to give them what they needed. She insisted they had everything she needed, but he couldn't deny his desires to give them more. He'd just find another way to do it.

But he agreed with Cassie. They needed him. They needed each other. Right now, they needed to find Alex.

Xavier gripped his wife's hand even firmer as they followed behind Maggie. The animal lover called out to her dogs. But silence greeted her at every turn. Until they came to the doors of the church.

Spin, the Irish Terrier who was a menace on wheels, poked his little head out of the open church doors. He cocked his head at his owner as though she were disturbing the peace. Then he turned and made his way back inside. Everyone followed the dog inside the church and down the hall.

And there they found her.

In the pulpit, in the makeshift manger that was always present, lay Alex. She was curled up sleeping on the hay. Her head lay against Star's patchy belly. Stevie and Sugar sat in a cocoon around her legs. Soldier sat up on his hind legs, parked in front of them all, as though he stood watch. Spin went over and sat down with his fellow comrade.

Each of the dogs opened one or two eyes and looked up at the humans as though offended at the intrusion. Meanwhile, Alex slept peacefully under their care.

No one stepped forward to disturb the sleeping girl or the dogs protecting her. Xavier tugged Cassie over to the pews, and they sat. The others made their way back out the doors as quietly as they'd come in leaving Xavier and his family alone.

"I'm sorry," he said after a while.

"I took my eye off her, too."

"No. For considering the contract work. It was the only way I could think of to provide for the two of you."

"I told you, all we need is you."

Xavier turned to his wife, the reason his heart beat, the reason he drew breath. "Cassie, I would never abandon you. I promised."

She tore her gaze away from Alex. When she faced her husband, she lifted an eyebrow. "I wasn't going to let you."

Xavier chuckled. The few punches that had landed in his belly earlier dissolved to flutters. His heart felt like it was both full and floating at the same time. That's what love felt like, a heavy lightness.

He leaned down to capture his wife's lips. Cassie met him more than halfway. Their lips brushed for a second before Xavier felt the need to deepen the kiss and claim what had always been and would forever be the very key to his soul.

"Eggs?"

Xavier chuckled as he turned from his wife to his waking daughter. "Hey, beautiful girl."

The dogs parted to make way for him. Xavier lifted Alex into his arms and returned with her to the pews to sit next to her mother.

Alex looked over at her mother and held out her arms. "Love?"

Cassie blinked. "What did you say, baby girl?"

"Love," Alex repeated opening and closing her hands to be picked up by her mother.

"I think that she thinks your name is love," said Xavier.

Now it was Cassie's turned to chuckle as she lifted Alex into her arms. "That would make sense. Since I always tell her I love you."

"Love." Alex squeezed her mother and kissed her cheek. "Eggs." She turned to her father and reached up to give him a kiss as well.

"I love you too, baby girl," Xavier said. "I love you both."

"And we love you," said Cassie.

"Love." Alex nodded and snuggled between her parents.

EPILOGUE

"Good morning, my love."

"Morning, Love. Breakfast?"

Cassie grinned down at her sleepy-eyed daughter as she stretched in her bed. In the last few months, Alex had added a few new words to her repertoire. Mom was one, but the little girl still insisted on calling Cassie *Love*. Cassie didn't mind at all. It was what she was surrounded by inside and out these days.

As she pulled the comforter off Alex to aid the kid in her getting-out-of-bed routine, Cassie stepped over Star who lay in front of Alex's night table, ever the guard dog.

"You want pancakes?" Cassie asked as she pulled a never been worn shirt from Alex's chest of drawers.

"Eggs."

Cassie knew Alex didn't want scrambled eggs or an omelet for breakfast. The liquid meat was still a textural issue for Alex.

No. Cassie knew that when Alex called out for eggs that her hubby was in the vicinity. And sure enough, her suspicion was confirmed a second later when his arms swooped Cassie up from behind.

"Xavier, careful."

"What?" he said, planting kissing along her neck. "I can't sweep the most amazing, beautiful, talented woman off her feet when I want to?"

"It's probably not a good idea for the next nine months."

Xavier froze. He carefully placed Cassie back down on her feet. He stepped away from her. Then stepped back, his gaze focused on her belly.

"Are you telling me?"

Cassie nodded.

"Are you sure?

She nodded again.

Xavier swooped her up again. Instead of chiding him, she laughed and relaxed into his embrace.

"Eggs!"

Xavier swooped Alex up to join the threesome. "You're going to be a big sister, kiddo."

Alex nodded as though she knew what her father meant. She probably did. The child was wise beyond her years. She just didn't show it in the conventional way.

"We're going to need a bigger house," said Xavier, looking around the large room as though the walls were closing in on him.

"Don't you start it. We have plenty of space here."

The man looked doubtful. This wasn't a battle Cassie was prepared to fight. She was too busy fighting morning sickness.

"Why are you back early?" she said in an effort to distract him. He usually didn't head back in from morning chores until Cassie and Alex were up and dressed and sitting down to breakfast.

"Ruhi's in labor. They're about to head to the hospital now."

With that message delivered, they filed out of the house and into the shared driveway of Sean and Ruhi's house. The very pregnant woman was waddling down the steps. Sean was at her side, carrying her overnight bag and looking like he wanted to swoop his wife up into his arms as well.

Cassie got in line to give her friend a hug before Ruhi ducked into the car. When Sean shut the passenger door, Cassie leaned in and stage-whispered to him, "Give me the signal if you want to run."

But Sean was as cool as a cucumber as always. He gave Cassie a peck on her cheek, then Alex a buss on the nose.

The group watched as the new parents pulled out of the drive and headed down the long and winding road that would lead them out of the Purple Heart Ranch and into town.

"This time tomorrow, there'll be another kid on the ranch," said Fran.

"This time in six months, there'll be yet another," said Dylan.

All eyes went to Maggie, who nodded, confirming the truth of her husband's words.

"You can add us to that playground," said Reed.

Sarai beamed in feigned annoyance, but the woman positively glowed as she stood inside her husband's embrace.

"Us too," said Xavier, breaking his and Cassie's news.

Fran looked to Eva, but the woman held up her hands.

"Don't even think about it, buddy," Eva said. "We've already got two to keep us busy for now."

"For now," Fran confirmed.

Chores were suspended as the group spent the rest of the day together waiting for news of the first baby of the ranch. As the sun went down, the news came. The girls cheered the loudest as their ranks increased. A new baby girl would come home to the ranch in a couple days.

She would be embraced by everyone who lived and visited here in this place of healing where five soldiers came to rehabilitate their wounds and wound up reviving their spirits by making convenient arrangements that turned into lasting love.

This may be the end of this squad's story, but a new squad is on their way to the ranch.
Follow the continuing story of the Wounded Warriors of the Purple Heart Ranch with
In Over IIis IIead
Book Six in the Brides of Purple Heart Ranch!

Shanae Johnson was raised by Saturday Morning cartoons and After School Specials. She still doesn't understand why there isn't a life lesson that ties the issues of the day together just before bedtime. While she's still waiting for the meaning of it all, she writes stories to try and figure it all out. Her books are wholesome and sweet, but her are heroes are hot and heroines are full of sass!

And by the way, the E elongates the A. So it's pronounced Shan-aaaaaaaa. Perfect for a hero to call out across the moors, or up to a balcony, or to blare outside her window on a boombox. If you hear him calling her name, please send him her way!

You can sign up for Shanae's Reader Group at http://bit.ly/ShanaeJohnsonReaders

Also By Shanae Johnson

The Brides of Purple Heart

On His Bended Knee

Hand Over His Heart

Offering His Arm

His Permanent Scar

Having His Back

In Over His Head

Always On His Mind

Every Step He Takes

In His Good Hands

Light Up His Life

Strength to Stand

The Rangers of Purple Heart

The Rancher takes his Convenient Bride

The Rancher takes his Best Friend's Sister

The Rancher takes his Runaway Bride

The Rancher takes his Star Crossed Love

The Rancher takes his Love at First Sight

The Rancher takes his Last Chance at Love

The Rebel Royals series

The King and the Kindergarten Teacher

The Prince and the Pie Maker

The Duke and the DJ

The Marquis and the Magician's Assistant

The Princess and the Principal